# THE PASSOVER PASSAGE

## BY SUSAN ATLAS

**TORAH AURA PRODUCTIONS**
**LOS ANGELES**

**Library of Congress Cataloging–in–Publication Data**

Atlas, Susan.
   The Passover passage / by Susan Atlas.
       p.   cm.
   Summary: A young girl spends the Passover holiday with her
grandparents on a sailboat learning about life, Judaism, and freedom.
   ISBN 0–933873–46–8 (pbk.)
   [1. Sailing—Fiction.  2. Sea stories.  3. Passover—Fiction.
4. Jews—United States—Fiction.]  I. Title.
PZ7.A8663Pas  1989                                    89–43121
[Fic]—dc20                                                  CIP
                                                             AC

First Edition


MANUFACTURED IN THE UNITED STATES OF AMERICA

Torah Aura Productions
4423 Fruitland Avenue
Los Angeles, California 90058
(800) BE-TORAH   (213) 585–7312

## DEDICATION

In memory of Gustav Marx, who loved the written word.

# ONE

THE SOUND OF THE JET ENGINES CHANGED SUDDENLY. Rebecca Able snapped her book shut and looked up in alarm. Was something wrong? This new sound had an urgent, straining quality to it. She pressed her face against the small window, looking for an answer. Everything appeared normal. The only difference was an apparent change of altitude. The plane was leaving the clear blue sky, heading swiftly into a dark blanket of clouds.

She slouched back into her seat. "Descending," she said to herself. She glanced at her watch. "It won't be much longer now."

Her ears suddenly began to hurt and she yawned a wide-open yawn to clear them. She heard a crackling noise and then felt much better.

Rebecca would have liked to lose herself in her book again, but too many thoughts and feelings crowded her mind.

There was excitement. She was flying to Florida to join her grandparents and sail to the Bahamas.

There was apprehension. She hadn't seen Grandma Maggie and Grandpa George in two years.

There was also a lingering sense of fear. This adventure could prove to be dangerous. She had heard the warnings over and over.

Grandmother Ida had nearly fainted when she learned about her granddaughter's plans. Rebecca could still hear the rising pitch of her voice as she struggled to control her panic.

"Cynthia! Are you mad? Have you lost your mind? You can't seriously be thinking of letting a mere child live on a boat. It's such a little boat—in the middle of the ocean. What about storms? What about sharks and whales? Please darling, don't let her go!"

They had gathered at the Able household for a marathon of hamentaschen baking.

Rebecca's mother stood very still. Only her stiffened back revealed any tension. Rebecca watched closely. How would she soothe grandmother's fears—fears that sprang from a lifelong dread of the ocean?

"You mustn't worry, Mother. Maggie and George have a lovely boat. It's perfectly safe. They've sailed all over the world in it."

"Sailing and safe are not words that belong together," Grandmother replied. "Why do something so dangerous? You have a beautiful, healthy daughter. Don't go looking for trouble."

"We're not looking for trouble …"

"So nu? You're looking maybe for adventure? Rebecca goes to summer camp every year. You send her horseback riding. She goes skiing in winter. Isn't that enough adventure?"

"No, Mother, we're not looking for adventure. This is a wonderful opportunity for Rebecca. So few people get the chance to do something unusual like this. Becca will be perfectly safe with David's parents."

Grandmother wiped the tears from her eyes and turned toward the table. Grandpa Jake was leaning back in his chair, playing with his coffee cup and chewing on an unlit cigar.

"Jacob! Tell your daughter that she can't do this! She always listens to you."

Grandpa Jake winked at Becca, who was standing just outside the kitchen door. He cleared his throat. He cleared his throat a second time.

"Please, Jacob. It's so dangerous! Please make her understand."

"Um-m-m," he muttered. "Um-m-m…well…yes, as you know. It's…well, you know how it is."

"Wonderful," Grandmother sobbed. "That was a big help."

Becca's throat felt tight and her eyes began to burn. She hated seeing her grandmother cry. Ida and Jake were her champions. Whatever she wanted, they bought for her. Whatever she wanted to eat, Grandmother baked for her. They came to every party. They sat with her, whenever she was sick. Becca felt sad and confused.

"You realize, of course, that Rebecca will be away during Pesach," Grandmother whispered as she struggled with her tears.

"Yes, Mother. I realize that vacation falls during the holiday. Rebecca will survive. There is a wonderful Pesach program at religious school. She'll participate in that before she leaves. Besides, I'm sure George and Maggie must celebrate Passover."

"How could they possibly hold a seder? That's the most ridiculous thing I've ever heard. Rebecca darling," she called. "Come here."

Becca stepped inside the door and hesitated.

"Sweetheart, you don't want to miss Pesach at home with all of the family, do you?"

Becca shrugged. She didn't want to stay and hear any more. Head lowered, she crept away to her room and shut her door.

In her nightstand was a neatly bundled collection of postcards. She spread them out on her bed and began to read.

"Dearest Becca, Our passage through the Panama Canal was very exciting. Our boat, the Diaspora, looked like a toy next to the ocean liners and freighters. We'll write when we can. Love and Kisses, Grandpa and Me."

"Dearest B, Sorry it's been so many weeks, but we've been at sea all this time. Coming at last to Easter Island was an amazing feeling. It was as if we had left the planet. Take care of little Alex for us. Grandpa and Me."

"Becca Dear, Bali is beautiful, but much too hot. We're getting homesick for Evanston and all our loved ones. Make plans for next spring. Grandpa and I want to take you sailing with us. How do the Bahamas sound? We'll call from Singapore. Love ,Grandma Maggie."

Rebecca turned the postcard over and gently touched the vibrant green of the jungle picture. This was the message that had started it all. The Bahamas had sounded wonderful then. They sounded wonderful now.

"Why can't Grandma Ida just be happy for me?" she sighed. "I want to go on this trip."

Still, there was a nagging doubt. Passover was her favorite holiday. Hanukkah made her uneasy. Too much competition with Christmas. The High Holidays were too solemn.

Passover was different. She loved getting the food ready. The dining room table was never more beautiful than at seder. All of the cousins were there, but no one was arguing or bragging about the number of presents they received. Even her little brother Alex was tolerable at Pesach. She did feel sad about missing it.

As Becca sat in her cramped seat, remembering her feelings that day, the quiet chime of the announcement bell brought her back to the present. The captain began to speak.

"Ladies and gentlemen, we are beginning our approach into Fort Lauderdale International Airport. If you haven't already done so, please fasten your seat belts. All trays are to be locked in the upright position. Anyone failing to follow these instructions will be asked to leave the aircraft immediately."

The captain's last statement brought a ripple of laughter through the cabin of the plane. Becca could hear the rustling of clothes being rearranged, followed by the sharp, metallic clicks of dozens of seat belts closing.

A little knot formed in her stomach. She sat back and took two deep breaths. Then she took two more. What would she do if her grandparents weren't at the airport to get her? What if her luggage wasn't on this plane? Becca felt a rising flood of panic. She pushed up her tray and twisted around to look for a flight attendant.

All of the crew members were busy. One was walking slowly down the aisle collecting leftover paper cups. Another was checking the overhead storage bins, securely closing all the doors. No one noticed Becca's anxious face, so she sat back in her seat and stared out the window.

The plane quickly left the bank of clouds behind. Now the city was clearly visible below. From her side of the plane, Becca could even see the ocean and the many hotels and marinas. As the plane flew even lower on its approach to the airport, she could see boats skimming across the water. Sleek powerboats raced along, leaving behind long rolling wakes. Here and there, a few stately sailboats were gliding over the shimmering surface. Becca found it hard to imagine herself on one of them. And yet, it was about to come true.

As the plane maneuvered toward the runway, the ocean disappeared from view. Becca watched the flaps on the wings spring upward. The engines began to whine. There was a slight bounce as the wheels touched down. They sped down the runway, past planes waiting to take off. Finally, the plane slowed to a controlled roll and eased gently up to the terminal. The captain thanked the passengers and asked them to remain seated until the plane came to a full stop.

As soon as they pulled up to the terminal, everyone stood up together. Becca shoved her book into her bright blue shoulder bag and slipped into the aisle. All around her was commotion. Packages were snatched from overhead compartments. Babies were crying and nearly everyone suddenly became noisy and festive. The aisle was jammed. She couldn't move an inch.

Becca looked out the airplane windows as she stood and waited. She marveled at the palm trees and the brilliantly colored hibiscus and bougainvillaea. There were flowers everywhere. She thought back to Chicago. When she had left that morning, there were scattered patches of snow. The grass was muddy brown. The flower gardens were lost under mounds of dead leaves. Even the pine trees seemed a dull, tired green.

Becca could hardly remember what eighty-degree weather felt like. She closed her eyes and thought about the sun baking her shoulders. She tried to imagine the sensation of the wind blowing over her wet bathing suit. She wiggled her toes in her shoes and tried to feel the tug and pull of sand on her feet.

Yes! She could really feel herself standing on the beach, looking out at the water. In her mind, she saw the many-colored windsurfers skimming the Lake Michigan waves.

A gentle nudge on her shoulder brought Becca back to the present. The line of people in front of her had begun to move. She gripped her bag firmly and headed out of the plane.

As Becca walked through the doors into the airport waiting area, she could see the other passengers scattering quickly. Some were joyously hugging friends and relatives. Others, mostly businessmen, were rushing down the long corridor to car rental booths and taxi stands. Crowds of students in bright T-shirts were excitedly discussing the busiest beaches. The sounds of many different languages echoed back and forth across the crowded airport.

Then Becca heard someone shouting her own name.

"Becca! Becca! Over here, darling!"

It was Grandma. She was standing with Grandpa at the edge of the crowd. They looked so tan and young. Grandma's short hair was bright blond from the constant sun. The few gray hairs blended in like silver streaks. Her quiet gray-blue eyes were shining. Grandpa looked just like...well, just like a sailor. His bald head was freckled with lots of sunburned pink spots. His arms were tanned to a dark, leathery brown and his hands were nicked and cut from working with the lines and metal fittings of the boat.

They were both wearing their white shirts with the four gold captains' bars on the shoulders. Becca had been so excited when they got their ranking. The captain's test was very difficult. Only a few husband-and-wife teams in the whole United States had ever qualified.

Her dad was exceptionally proud of them. He framed their graduation photo and hung it in the living room. Grandma Ida shuddered each time she saw it and moved it to the den, whenever she could.

Becca practically flew across the lobby when she saw them. Grandma threw her arms around her and they twirled together in a tight little circle of joy.

"Rebecca," she said when they came to a stop. "You're as tall as I am. And so grown-up. What happened to my little girl?"

Becca laughed. It was true. This past year of junior high had brought big changes. She wasn't the little girl her grandparents remembered. Her brown hair was long and swept back. She had carefully framed her dark eyes with liner and added a touch of shadow. And she had grown very tall. Most of the boys barely came to her shoulders. Mom kept saying the boys would catch up. Becca certainly hoped so. Her cousin Josh's bar mitzvah party had been a disaster! She had felt like a giant with all those short dancing partners.

Grandpa reached out to pull her ear. It had always been his special greeting to her.

"What's this?" he asked. "Earrings on my girl?"

"I've had pierced ears since second grade," she replied. "Don't you remember?"

"Your grandmother doesn't have pierced ears."

"I know. She's probably the last person in the world without them."

"I don't have a hole in my ear. You know, Miss B, when we were in New Guinea, everyone had holes through their noses. I think you would look great with a bone right through here." He grabbed her playfully and pretended to run his finger through the front of her nose.

Becca squirmed away laughing. "No! No! No!" she gasped through her laughter. "Just ears. That's all I'm allowed to pierce. You can check with Mom and Dad."

"Hey," Grandpa said. "I'm the oldest one in this family. I don't have to check with anyone." Then he winked and teased some more.

"That's not a very big bag. I guess you must have only packed a bathing suit."

"Really Grandpa! I have another suitcase."

"Well then, let's go get it. We have a lot of preparation on the boat before we begin our sail. We leave at midnight."

"Midnight!" Becca gasped. "Really?"

Grandma nodded. "We'll be sailing by moonlight tonight."

# TWO

THE TAXI RIDE FROM THE AIRPORT TO THE MARINA was hot and sticky, but Rebecca didn't mind. After the long winter, the heat felt good. As they crept along in the heavy mid-day traffic, she watched out the window, fascinated by the strange, tropical scenery.

She had been in Florida many years before. It was on the occasion of her uncle's wedding. She had been the flower girl.

Her memories of that trip were vague. She remembered waves rolling in along the shore, and walking with her plastic bucket. She remembered looking for shells. In Dad's photo album, there were pictures of her at a dolphin show and at DisneyWorld, but she couldn't actually recall having been to those places.

Now, looking out at the wildly painted homes, each surrounded by brilliant flowers, Becca was overwhelmed by their exotic appearance. She turned to her grandparents and said in amazement, "This doesn't look like America at all!"

"You know, dear," her grandmother said, "you've traveled just about 1500 miles, since you left home this morning. If this was Europe or Southeast Asia, you would have flown over many different countries in that distance."

"I know that," Becca replied, "but I didn't think that the houses and office buildings and everything would be so different.

"Look at that house over there," she said, pointing out the window. "No one up north would paint their house lavender with lime green shutters. And look!" she pointed at another home. "There's a  bright yellow one, and the one next to it is turquoise!" Everything looked so foreign, but it looked right. Maybe the brightly colored houses would seem odd in Illinois, but down here, they fit.

As the taxi traveled closer to the ocean, Becca could feel the cooler air. She began to pick up the distinctive odor of the seashore. It was made up of seaweed and clams and dead fish, all baking in the noon sun. It really wasn't an unpleasant smell, just unfamiliar.

She remembered the time she'd taken a Florida cousin to the cheese factory near her home. Poor Betsy had run out of the building holding her nose.

"I guess it's what you're used to," Becca mused.

Soon they came to a bridge over the intercoastal waterway.

"Look now," Grandpa said suddenly. "Can you see the port?"

There, on the right, was Port Everglades. It was huge, very busy and very noisy. There were freighters and commercial fishing boats. Along the docks, several mammoth ocean liners waited for passengers. A steady stream of small pleasure boats passed under the bridge they were crossing. The oily odor of diesel fumes lingered in the humid air. It made Becca sneeze.

The taxi bounced along, and just minutes later the open ocean lay in front of them.

"Can you hear the breakers yet?" her grandmother asked.

Becca strained to hear the sound of the waves on the shore, but the noise of the wheezing taxi was all she could discern.

"Can you hear them?" she asked.

"When you live on a boat, it seems as if you can always hear the waves breaking. It doesn't matter where you are," Grandma replied.

"Yeah," Grandpa added, "and you can feel the ground rolling like a boat. Even on dry land."

"No you can't!" Becca protested. "How can you feel the ground rolling?" Grandpa was surely teasing again. She looked at Grandma for support.

"It's true, Rebecca," Grandma said. "It's very strange, but it's true. It has to do with the liquid in your inner ear. At first, every motion of the boat will bother you, but once you've gotten used to it, you'll find that you feel unsteady on solid ground."

Becca was unconvinced. "I can tell you this much," she declared. "I'm not going to get seasick! Dad and I go on all the rides at the fair. I love the roller coaster. Mom has to hold my hand, because she's afraid, but I'm not. And I never get sick."

"There's no reason that you should," Grandpa told her. "The waters around the Bahamas are shallow and smooth. Why, we'll be sailing a whole day across water that's only eight feet deep."

"The pool at school is deeper than that," Becca said, very much surprised. "How can that be?"

"Well, the islands here are great big sandbars. That's why there are so many shipwrecks in the area. In fact, we have to be especially careful. Our boat draws nearly seven feet."

"What do you mean?" Becca laughed. She imagined the boat drawing pictures of feet with an enormous crayon.

"I mean that there's almost seven feet of keel under the water line. It gives the boat greater stability, but in shallow water, we could get stuck."

When the taxi thumped to a stop at the next light, Becca could finally see the marina. Long T-shaped piers thrust out into the harbor. The intercoastal entered one end and exited the other. It looked like a regular highway. Boats were moving in steady lines in either direction.

As they approached their destination, Rebecca saw that most of the boats were fishing boats—sportfishing boats. Their hulls were shiny and sleek, but enormously high lookout towers gave them an awkward appearance. Great big fishing poles bristled from their transoms like tail feathers.

Past the rows and rows of sports boats were several piers filled with elegant power yachts.

"They're beautiful," Becca said. "I thought boats had little round windows. These look like they have big picture windows."

"That's what they are," Grandpa told her. "Those yachts have living rooms that are bigger than the one in your house. They have dining rooms with cooks and waitresses. The bedrooms have queen-size beds and private baths. Some even have built-in spas."

Becca's big brown eyes grew wide with amazement. "They have all those things inside a boat? That's almost like being at a fancy hotel."

"Better," Grandpa said. "Hotels can't travel around."

"Look!" he exclaimed next. "We've reached our pier."

The taxi pulled up to the one pier that had only sailboats. Becca could see small groups of lean, tanned sailors gathered around. They were clad in cut-off jeans and torn shirts. No starched uniforms like on the yachts. The sailors lounged against the posts, chatting, just shooting the breeze.

Curiosity and excitement took hold of Rebecca. She pulled open the door of the taxi and jumped out.

"Come on, Grandma" she said. "I can't wait to see your boat!"

She grabbed her shoulder bag and Grandpa took her suitcase. They started down the pier to their boat.

# THREE

MAKING THEIR WAY DOWN THE WIDE WOODEN pier took a certain amount of agility. The path was blocked not only by the lounging sailors, but also by their scampering dogs. Children's toys were scattered here and there. Many of the boats had water hoses and electrical cords snaking across the pier to the utility outlets, as well.

Becca glanced at each boat as they passed. A frown creased her forehead. Something was not right.

"Grandma," she whispered, tugging on her grandmother's arm. "Do we use sleeping bags on top of the boat?"

Grandma laughed. Still, it was a reasonable question. It was mid-tide and they had to look down to see the boats. From where they stood, only the padded seats of the cockpits and the smooth decks were visible.

"No, no." she replied. "You'll have your own cabin below. We have bathrooms ..."

"Heads," Grandpa corrected her. "In boats, they're called heads."

"Yes, dear," Grandma said. "The boat has two heads, both with showers. And we have a very nice kitchen ..."

"Galley," Grandpa chimed in.

"Galley," Grandma repeated. "And there's a salon where we eat and watch TV."

"TV! Can I watch the videos?"

"Videos!" Grandpa bellowed in mock indignation. "No way!"

"Most of the places we'll be anchored have no television reception," Grandma explained. "When we're at home in Key Largo, we can get the local broadcasts. When we're cruising, we don't turn the television on very often."

Becca shrugged. "That's okay," she said. "I was just curious."

Just then Grandpa stopped and pointed. "There she is! There's our Diaspora!"

The Diaspora was different from all the other sailboats. Up and down the pier, Becca could see a forest of aluminum masts. Diaspora's was a burnished gold. Instead of having textured decks of white fiberglass, she had gray-brown natural teak. The other boats had portholes of shiny stainless steel. The Diaspora's were brass, with a faint patina of green.

"She looks like a boat from a different time," Becca said. She's even more beautiful than in your photos."

"That's why we love her so much," Grandma said. "Inside, she's state-of-the-art. She even has a microwave oven and radar. But outside, she's old-fashioned and romantic."

"That's right," Grandpa chortled. "And old-fashioned boats need to be scrubbed down and polished every day. That's why we've invited you along. It's the duty of the youngest crew member to shine the brass. All of it. Every day!"

"Not very likely," Becca replied, and began to tickle him.

"Stop! Stop!" he shouted. "I'll throw you off the pier with the seaweed and dead fish."

He wrapped an arm around her waist and lifted her up. While she struggled and shrieked with laughter, he marched down the pier until they came to the side of the Diaspora. He put her down with a grunt.

"You're getting too big for this," he complained.

Becca stopped laughing and paused to examine the sailboat. Her eyes swept its length, admiring every detail.

Hanging off the stern was a tiny wooden dinghy. Next came the cockpit, with its wheel of gleaming wood. The pilot house wall held a fascinating row of nautical instruments. Each line was coiled carefully and laid in place along the deck. The final touch was an intricately carved panel edging the entire boat and running out along the extended bowsprit.

"Give me your hand," Grandpa said to her. "Getting on board can be tricky."

"I can do it myself," Becca answered.

"Well, okay," he replied. "But if you slip and fall, it's a long way down to the water."

"I know," she said, "and I can do it. Really I can!"

Becca waited while he opened the gate in the low guard railing. Then she carefully hopped from the pier onto the boat.

"Nothing to it," she said to her grandfather, as he and Grandma followed her onto the boat.

"Welcome to the Diaspora," Grandma said solemnly.

"Why did you name her that?" Rebecca asked.

"For thousands of years...since Babylonia, and ever after," Grandma replied, "Jews have lived in the Diaspora. In exiled communities. Scattered over the globe. Diaspora comes from a Greek word, which means 'dispersion.' But no matter where we lived, if it was for a year or a thousand years, we never forgot who we were and why we were different from our neighbors. "When your grandfather and I are sailing, we're away from our loved ones. But we never forget."

"And we never forget," Grandpa added, "that Judaism teaches we have a responsibility to repair the world."

"Tikkun olam," Grandma interjected.

"Tikkun olam," he repeated. "Do you know what that means?"

"No," she admitted.

"Think about it for a minute. What is melech ha'olam?"

"King of the universe," Becca answered. "Every prayer has that phrase."

"So the word olam refers to everything, everyone."

"Yes."

"You see, when we talk about our covenant with God, we aren't talking about benefits only for ourselves. Our part of the agreement is to do the mitzvot, the commandments, and make all of the world a better place. Tikkun olam!"

"You don't have to leave home to fulfill the covenant," Grandma added, "but Grandpa and I have always felt that we wanted to know and understand those elements of the world that were foreign to us. We feel that traveling actually increases our commitment to Judaism and helps us to be more effective in our efforts to help others."

Becca nodded in surprised silence. She couldn't recall ever hearing her grandparents speak out about their Judaism before. Maybe she had been too young. Maybe she had been too interested in the gifts they had brought home for her.

Now, as she watched Grandma remove the padlock from the main hatch, she noticed a beautiful brass mezuzah attached to the framework.

"You have a mezuzah!" she exclaimed.

"This is our home," Grandpa said, "and that's as close as we come to a doorpost. Go on down. We'll show you around."

The stairs were very narrow, very steep and curving. It felt more like climbing down a ladder. Becca scrambled down them, then looked around in delight. Below deck, the boat appeared much larger.

The wood-paneled pilot house, with its inside helm, was more than a refuge from the weather. It was a salon, with a dining room table. It was a den with many bookshelves. It was a living room with a couch and chairs, covered in deep blue velour. It even had an Oriental rug on the floor.

"It's beautiful," Becca gasped. "Does every boat have a pilot house like this?"

"No," Grandpa replied. "Not very many. Most are much more utilitarian and few have the inside wheel."

"That must come in handy."

"To tell you the truth, I prefer to stay on deck even in bad weather. I feel as though I have more control over the situation. Still, it's nice to know it's here if I need it."

"Come over here, dear," Grandma called. "Let me show you the galley and your cabin."

Becca moved forward and down a step. She looked out the small, round porthole and could see the pilings of the pier. To her left was the boat's tiny but efficient galley.

There was a deep refrigerator set in under the counter and a freezer unit that could be reached by lifting up a door in the far corner. There was a small sink and a funny three-burner stove that swung back and forth on gimbals.

Becca gave the stove a gentle push and watched it rock.

"Why is the stove loose?" she asked.

"That's so I can cook even when the waves are rocking the boat," Grandma explained. "The stove actually will stay steady because of gravity. I can clamp the pots and pans onto the burners, then I don't have to worry about food spilling."

Becca nodded. That made sense to her. She reached up and touched the controls of the microwave sitting above the stove.

"Pretty fancy for a boat," she teased.

"Maybe," Grandma said. "But I'd rather be swimming than cooking meals all afternoon.

"Besides," she added. "If you think a microwave oven is fancy, take a look at Grandpa's toys."

Becca turned around and looked at the navigation station on the other side of the boat. The entire wall was filled with digital readouts and push-button gizmos. There was a radar screen, a stereo music system and two different microphones for calling between boats or to shore.

On the desk was a chart showing the area from Ft. Lauderdale to West End in the Bahamas. On the chart the area seemed immense. It was crisscrossed with lines and every available space was filled with numbers.

"That's my road map," Grandpa told her. "I bet you thought we could just go ahead and sail across any way we wanted to."

"I did," Becca confessed. "This looks terribly complicated."

"It is. That's why boats go down in the islands all the time. Their captains don't bother to find out about the bottom conditions or about all the tiny outcroppings of rocks and uninhabited islands. They call them cays down here, exactly like the Florida Keys."

"Will it be dangerous for us?" Becca asked.

"It could be quite an adventure if the wind isn't just right," Grandpa replied. "Anyway, a nighttime sail is always pretty exciting. Now quit asking questions and get your stuff stowed in your cabin. There's still plenty of work before we sail."

"Here's your cabin, honey," Grandma said. "It's in the front of the boat, the bow."

Becca went up a step. On her right was a door. She pulled it open. There was a tiny sink and a small round toilet. Next to them was a standing shower with two sets of faucets.

"I guess this is a head," Becca said, "but why are there double faucets in the shower?"

"We can carry only a limited amount of fresh water," Grandma explained, looking over Becca's shoulder. "That means we have to use it carefully. You'll wash up with a special soap and sea water from the first faucet. Then you'll rinse with the fresh water from the second."

Becca backed out of the head and took another step up into her cabin. Cabin was probably not the right word for it. It was more like a large closet. The bed was perched up another two steps and had drawers under it. In order to fit into the boat's pointed bow, the berth was wide at the top and very narrow at the bottom.

Still, she was thrilled. Her cabin was so cozy and private. The quilt was many shades of blue with white sailboats across it. The pillows were big and plump and there was a small hatch directly above the bed. Becca patted the pillows and lifted up the hatch. Far above her, she could see the lines and rigging running up the mast. She would have loved to lie there and watch the clouds, but there was work to be done.

Becca quickly stowed away her clothes. She took her empty nylon suitcase, folded it and slid it into the shoe locker. She closed everything tightly. Grandma had warned her that the drawers could slide open while they were sailing. She needed to be extra careful.

That chore completed, she left her little cabin and made her way back through the boat. Her grandparents' cabin was in the stern, behind the salon. Grandma was inside, folding towels and swimsuits.

Their cabin was not much larger than Becca's,but there was room for a rug on the floor. The bed was wider and lower. It fit into the space beneath the cockpit. There was a tiny head right inside the cabin. Becca looked around thoughtfully, then decided she liked her own berth better. There wasn't a hatch in this cabin.

"I'm ready to go," Becca told her grandmother. "I've put everything away. What do we do now?"

"Well," Grandma said. "I have a long shopping list. We won't be around any markets for a great deal of the time. We'll have to put on enough supplies to be self-sufficient."

She reached for her purse and rummaged inside.

"Yes," she said. "Here it is. Grandpa and I spent an hour last night writing down everything we're going to need. Let me find my sunglasses and we can get started."

# FOUR

EVEN THOUGH THERE WAS A SMALL GROCERY STORE at the marina, Becca and her grandparents took a taxi to a larger supermarket in town.

"Finding supplies for Pesach won't be any problem in Fort Lauderdale," Grandma said. "There's a very large Jewish community here. It's a sure bet, however, that none of them shop at the marina. We won't find any matzah there."

"It's too bad we won't be having a seder," Becca replied.

"Says who?" Grandpa snapped. "We have seder every year, no matter where we are—no matter if it's just Maggie and me."

"Doesn't it seem strange with only two of you?"

"Don't get me wrong," he answered. "We'd prefer to be with the whole family. That makes it extra special. But Passover is too important to be ignored. As it is written, 'Once we were slaves in Pharaoh's Egypt.' Now, Pharaoh is gone, but we still persevere. So we take out the Haggadah, and have a seder every Passover. Without fail."

"Can you get matzah everywhere? Last year you were in Indonesia."

Grandma laughed. "We couldn't find it there, so I made my own. It turned out pretty awful, but we used it anyway."

"We made matzah at Sunday School, but the rabbi told us we couldn't use it during Pesach."

"There are Jews all over the world who don't have the luxury of buying 'Kosher for Passover' matzah. That's not the important part. It's the remembering that's important. Because we remember living in slavery, we must help others who are still enslaved. That's why we have celebrated Pesach and the seder for many thousands of years. We thank God for our freedom and for the mitzvot."

"I know that there are countries where laws are much stricter than at home, but I didn't think there was slavery anymore."

"I guess that depends on your definition of slavery," Grandpa replied.

Becca frowned. She looked over at Grandma.

"I don't think I understand," she said.

"Slavery can come in many forms," Grandma answered. "Slavery can be the loss of freedom that comes from poverty or lack of education. Or, if you are thrown in jail for expressing your opinions, that is surely being enslaved."

"That's right, Becca," Grandpa said. "One of our most compelling commandments is the freeing of captives. Perhaps that's why so many Jews choose to be doctors or teachers or lawyers. Each of those professions focuses on freeing people from the problems that can enslave their bodies and minds."

"But that still doesn't mean it's okay to eat non-kosher matzah. I know that Grandma Ida would be very upset if she found out. She says you can't really be Jewish if you ignore the laws for living, the halachah." Becca felt uneasy and confused by the conflicting opinions of her grandparents.

"I don't agree," Grandpa said quietly. "Judaism is so vital…its ideals are so universal…you can spend Passover in the Himalayas, drinking yak-butter tea with Buddhist monks. It would in no way diminish your commitment to Judaism. That's why we've survived for four thousand years, while all of the others have vanished."

Becca thought over his words in silent contemplation. She had always thought that Judaism was such a complicated religion. Suddenly it seemed so simple, so straightforward. She promised herself to never again let ceremony prevail over substance.

It was Grandma who finally broke the silence. She hauled the grocery list out of her purse.

"No matter how carefully I shop," she said, "it always seems that I've forgotten something crucial. Maybe I'll do a better job this time. Can I count on your help, Rebecca?"

"I'll try," Becca replied. "Mom says I'm a terrible shopper. I'm always picking out candy bars and big boxes of breakfast cereal."

"We don't allow candy bars on our boat," Grandpa said with a straight face. "All you can have to eat is uncooked fish and coconuts that float out from the cays. Your grandmother is a regular tyrant. She won't even let us have salt on our potato chips."

Grandma looked lovingly at him. "If I let him," she said, "your grandfather would fill all the cabinets with cookies and we'd have nothing but ice cream in the freezer."

In the end, they managed to remember everything. They completely filled up two shopping carts with their supplies. They bought chicken and ground beef and steaks. They bought matzah and matzah meal, but they also bought pasta and bread and a big bag of rice. They bought parsley and horseradish for the seder plate, along with enough fresh fruits and vegetables to fill an entire grocery bag. They bought some kosher wine and many gallons of bottled water. They bought cheeses and salamis. They bought nuts for the charoset. Grandpa stocked up on paper goods and garbage bags. Becca added a box of granola bars and a half gallon of chocolate swirl ice cream.

The taxi ride home was uneventful, though somewhat uncomfortable. Becca wasn't sure which she disliked most, sitting sideways in the stuffy hot taxi or holding the bag with the ice cream, which nearly froze the tops of her legs right off.

In order to lug all their bags of groceries down the pier, they had to borrow a big wooden cart from the dock master. Even with that, it was quite a difficult task. Grandpa pulled with the handle, while Becca and Grandma walked on either side, guarding against an avalanche of brown paper bags.

At last, giggling and breathless, they arrived at the Diaspora.

"Here's how we'll manage the next step," Grandpa instructed them. "Grandma, you go below and wait at the foot of the stairs. Becca, you're going to stand on deck and get the bags from me. Then you'll carry them over to the stairs. When the cart is empty, I'll return it to the dock master while you girls get everything put away. Is everybody ready? Okay, let's get to it!"

In no time at all, they had ferried the bags from the dock to the tiny galley deep inside the sailboat. Becca watched for a moment as Grandpa made his way back down the pier. Then she hurried below deck to help her grandmother.

Storing away the contents of nine large grocery sacks was not very easy. Grandma had her shelves packed three items high and two deep. The things that needed to be frozen were placed in a brightly colored plastic basket and lowered with a long metal handle into the freezer compartment.

"Where are you going to put the bottled water?" Becca asked. She couldn't see any possible spot in the galley.

"Bottled water, paper towels, tissue and garbage bags go under your bunk, Rebecca," Grandma answered.

"Under my bunk? But how?"

"There isn't a wasted space on this boat," Grandma said. "Come with me and I'll show you what I mean."

Becca followed her grandmother up the narrow steps leading to the forward cabin. She watched from the hallway as Grandma lifted the edge of the bunk platform, revealing a large chest-like storage area beneath.

"Hand me all that extra stuff, dear," Grandma said.

Becca passed everything forward, one item at a time, and watched amazed as each disappeared into that cavernous space. They finished just as Grandpa swung down the steep steps into the salon. He tossed his floppy canvas hat onto a chair and rubbed his bald head.

"Well, we're ready to sail. I've paid for the water and the diesel fuel. The only line still connected is for the electricity." He looked at his watch. "Six o'clock. Let's get a sandwich at the stand, then we can come back here and get some sleep. At least we'll have a few hours before we go."

At the center of the marina, up a slight hill, there was a little refreshment stand. The three of them took their food and drinks and sat at a table with a yellow striped umbrella. The heat of the day had subsided and a slight breeze fanned the air.

"Why are we sailing at midnight?" Becca asked.

"We have to enter West End at high tide or we'll go aground in their harbor," Grandpa replied. "It takes around sixteen hours to get there and high tide is at five o'clock tomorrow. Therefore, we leave at midnight."

Becca nodded and then she yawned. Even though it was still early in the evening, her eyelids were growing heavy. It had been a long day. She had left home at four o'clock that morning.

She gazed sleepily out at the ocean. The seagulls looked nearly pink against the dark blue sky to the east. Far in the distance, she could see the towers of the fishing boats coming home.

"Let's go get some sleep," she said and stood up.

# FIVE

ECCA AWOKE ABRUPTLY TO THE SOUND OF AN engine's rumbling cough. At first, she was confused. Where was she? Then the memories of the day swept back to her mind. The Diaspora! It was time to leave for the Bahamas.

Becca rolled onto her back and gazed up out of the hatch. The moon was directly overhead, veiled by clouds. The flags on the rigging flapped frantically in a heavy wind. She wondered when the wind had come up. There had been only a gentle breeze when she fell asleep.

"Time to get up Becca," Grandma called out.

Becca leaned over and stuck her head out of the cabin. Her grandmother was dressed in long pants and a windbreaker.

"It's chilly, so you'd better dress warmly," she said.

Becca slipped out of bed and wrestled with the stubborn drawer. It finally opened. She took out jeans and a jacket and pulled them on. She pushed aside her sandals and found her sneakers.

"Here's your life vest," Grandma said. "We never sail at night without them."

Becca was about to protest. Then she saw that it was not one of those awkward orange contraptions that made her feel as if she was being suffocated. Instead, it was a handsome red and blue striped vest that zipped up the front. She put hers on and felt comfortably reassured. Grandpa had said that a night sail could be an adventure. That meant it could be dangerous as well.

Grandma put on her own vest and handed the largest one to Becca.

"Here. Take this one up to Grandpa. I'm going to finish battening down all the hatches."

Becca climbed up the stairs and gave the vest to her grandfather. He was standing at the wheel, reading the wind gauges. They were glowing red in the dark. Silently, he took the vest from Becca. He never even looked up at her. Becca felt uneasy and hurried below.

Grandma was standing on the couch in the salon, cranking the handle of the window hatch until it squealed. Becca looked around. Everything was tightly shut. The potted plants were sitting in the galley sink. Every loose item had been stored away securely.

Becca looked carefully at her grandmother's face. Grandma's teeth were clenched. Worried lines crossed her forehead. Becca felt a knot of fear growing in her stomach.

"What's wrong?" she asked.

"Hopefully nothing," Grandma replied.

That answer did not satisfy Becca. "What could be wrong?" she asked this time. "Grandpa looks worried too."

"It's probably going to be just fine," she said. "We are a little concerned over this wind. The weather report indicated the wind would be gentle out of the south, but it's quite heavy from the north. It's supposed to switch within the hour and become favorable. The problem is that we can't delay. We leave now or we wait until tomorrow night."

"Maggie!" Grandpa bellowed from above. "Check the weather once more. The engine's warmed up and it's time for a decision."

Grandma walked over to the nav station and turned on the weather channel. The news was the same. Clearing skies and winds switching to the south and decreasing.

"Let's go!" Grandma yelled up at Grandpa. "The weather should be fine before we get into the open ocean."

Becca's fear turned instantly into excitement. She sprinted up the stairs and plopped herself on the padded seat of the cockpit storage bench.

"Can I help?" she asked her grandfather. "Can I help on the lines or with the steering wheel?"

"You can help by staying out of the way," he replied. "Once we're past the piers, you can hold the charts and the flashlight for Grandma. She's the pilot whenever we're in harbor."

As if on cue, Grandma emerged from inside and took over the wheel.

"Here's my plan," she told Grandpa. "I'll back straight out until the bow is clear. Then I'll swing the stern to starboard. That's the right side," she explained to Becca. "Then I'll start forward to the channel. Is that okay?"

"Fine," he replied. "I'll release the stern spring line and guide us away from the pier with the bowline. Are you ready?"

"Ready," Grandma said. Grandpa released the stern line and hurried to the bow. The Diaspora shifted smoothly into reverse and began slipping away from the dock.

Suddenly, a gust of wind caught the stern and slammed the boat back into its berth. There was an awful sound of splintering wood and a screech of metal wire being stretched beyond endurance. Grandma instantly threw the boat into neutral.

"Oh no!" she groaned under her breath. Becca twisted around to see where the damage had occurred.

"It's the dinghy," she told Grandma. "It's caught on the rigging of the sailboat next to us."

Grandpa secured the bowline and hurried to the stern.

"Now what happened?" he yelled above the wind.

"It was a gust," Grandma yelled back. "The wind threw us sideways in the berth. The dinghy's hooked on the rigging of the Wanderer."

The Wanderer was a rented charter boat that shared the dock space with the Diaspora. Grandpa hung over the stern to examine the damage and assess the situation.

The transom of their little dinghy had a large gouge near the outboard motor and it was snagged tightly in the rigging of the other boat. Grandpa reached out and tried to pull the dinghy loose. It wouldn't budge. The wind gusted again and the side of the Diaspora smacked into the charter boat with a resounding crash.

Now there was more yelling. The crew of the other boat had been rather rudely awakened. Two sleepy men angrily climbed up onto the deck of their boat.

"What the blazes are you doing out here in the middle of the night?" they demanded to know.

Grandma, the peacemaker, apologized fervently. The sight of her desperate and worried face softened their annoyance. Soon everyone was working together to free the two boats. There was no damage to the Wanderer, and the dinghy could be repaired.

This time the departure from the pier went smoothly. Extra hands, helping to steady the backward progress of the boat, made a big difference. As the Diaspora eased forward and headed for the channel, Grandpa finished securing the lines and hurried to the cockpit.

"Let's have a look at those charts," he said to Becca.

He clicked on the flashlight and studied them carefully. Then he checked his watch. It was twelve forty-five.

"It's a good thing that we left ourselves some extra time. Crashing around into other boats wasn't part of the plan. Now listen, just ahead is a big turn in the waterway. Remember to stay to the left of the red channel markers or we could get stuck."

He handed the charts and the flashlight back to Becca.

"It's important for you to pay attention," he warned her. "When Grandma needs to check the depths, you'll have to turn the light on right away and hold it steady. I'm going out on the bowsprit and watch for shallow water."

"Won't you need the flashlight?" Becca asked him.

"No. The beam would only reflect off the surface of the water. I'm better off by the light of the moon."

"Keep an eye on the depth indicator," Grandma told her. "It's that readout in the middle of the instrument panel. We need seven feet. If you keep telling me the depth, I won't have to look away from the channel markers."

Slowly and carefully, they made their way down the waterway. Grandpa used his arms like a traffic cop to point out the best path through the shallow water. Becca called out the depths. Several times the indicator read six feet, but the wind-whipped waves swept beneath them and they missed hitting the bottom.

As they eased cautiously into the turn, Grandpa pointed to the right from his perch on the bowsprit.

Grandma jumped up onto the seat to get a better look.

"That's wrong," she muttered. "We should be to port of the marker, not to the starboard."

"Six feet," Becca called out.

"Six feet," she said again, then the glowing red number switched to five.

The boat gave a shudder and stopped moving.

Grandma pushed the throttle wide open. The engine roared and water churned in great muddy swirls behind them. But the boat did not move. Becca held her breath and watched fearfully.

Now Grandma threw the engine into reverse. Again it roared into life. The waves beat at the bow and there was a momentary feeling of motion. Then nothing.

"Damn," Grandma said softly and dropped her forehead onto the wheel.

Grandpa walked back to the cockpit. He looked old, tired and defeated. When he saw Becca's frightened face, he forced a smile.

"Thing's aren't so bad," he teased her. "We're only a half mile from the pier. You can swim back and get help, can't you?"

Becca stood up and looked back down the channel.

"I don't think I can swim that far," she said. "What are we going to do? Are we going to be stuck here forever?"

"Well," Grandpa replied, "we can sit here until the next high tide or we can get on the VHF radio and call for the towboat. What do you think we should do?"

"Will the towboat come in the middle of the night?" she asked. "Won't we have to wait until morning?"

"I don't know. I haven't ever needed a tow before. I guess that's hard to believe, considering all the problems we've had tonight."

"At least we're even," Grandma chided him quietly. "I got us hooked on the other boat and you put us on a sandbar."

Grandpa started to protest. Then he stopped himself.

"It's late," he said. "I think we won't discuss it any further."

Grandma nodded her agreement and handed him the VHF unit from its holder next to the wheel. He switched it on.

"Port Everglades. Port Everglades. Port Everglades. This is the Diaspora," he called, then waited for about fifteen seconds.

"Port Everglades. Port Everglades. Port Everglades. This is the Diaspora," he called again.

"Diaspora, this is Port Everglades Coast Guard. Go to channel 68," an answer crackled back over the VHF.

Grandpa changed channels, then continued.

"Port Everglades, we're aground at red buoy number 12. Can we get a tow right away? We're on a tight schedule."

"Diaspora, what are your dimensions?"

"We're a forty-three foot cutter, with a six-feet four-inch draft."

"Okay Diaspora. We'll contact a commercial tow for you. Can you keep your vessel from turning sideways and blocking the channel?"

No problem, Everglades. Thanks. We'll be looking for the tow. Diaspora out."

Grandpa replaced the VHF radio in its holder, but left it on "Receive".

"We should be monitoring the open channel anyway," he said.

"Go sit down." He patted Grandma on the shoulder. "I'll keep us steady until the tow gets here."

Grandma plopped down beside Becca.

"Are you tired, honey?" she asked. "You don't have to sit up with us. Why don't you go lie down in your cabin?"

"Oh no Grandma," Becca protested. "I want to see the towboat. And I'm not tired. Really I'm not."

Grandma snuggled her and smoothed her wind-blown hair. "This is a good omen," she said. "We'll get rid of all our problems tonight and from now on, the trip will be perfect. How does that sound?"

Becca laughed. "Okay," she said. "But tonight's trip will sure be a good story to tell everyone back home."

"Everyone but Ida," Grandpa reminded her. "If she heard about all these mishaps, she'd never let you come with us again."

Becca chuckled. "Poor Mom. Grandma insisted on coming with us to the airport, then she fussed the whole way. She said she won't sleep until I'm home."

"Too bad she's so terrified of the water," Grandpa said. "I bet Jake would love to come sailing with us."

After only a few more minutes, the towboat came chugging down the channel. It pulled alongside.

"Hello!" Grandpa called. "Thanks for coming out so quickly."

"No problem," the man called back. "No one else is sailing around in this gale."

He was right. Instead of settling down, the wind had continued to rise. Becca felt chilled even with her jacket on.

"Where are you heading for?" the man called out.

"West End," Grandpa replied. "We have to go into their harbor at high tide."

"You'll be under way a bit late, but with this wind, you should be moving fast enough. Do you still want to try for it?"

Grandpa looked at Grandma. "Do we turn back?" he asked.

"No way," Grandma replied. "We've gotten this far. I'm sure the rest of the trip will be fine."

"The wind's still from the north," he said.

"It will switch," she told him. "Let's get going."

Grandpa turned back to the towboat captain.

"We're going to keep going," he told him.

"Well, good luck," the man replied. "The tow costs seventy-five dollars. In advance."

Grandpa paid the captain while the two boats were side by side. He took the two heavy lines from the tow boat and walked forward as the other boat pulled ahead. He secured them to the bow cleats of the Diaspora. Then he gave a "go ahead" sign with his hand.

The tow boat's powerful engines began churning through the water.

Grandpa hurried back to the cockpit. He pushed the throttle open on the Diaspora. Nothing seemed to be happening. Suddenly, the sailboat began to slide forward. There was the sound of the keel dragging through the sand. At last, she pulled free of the bottom.

Grandpa pulled back on the throttle and gave the wheel to Grandma. He hurried to the bow to throw off the lines. All three of them waved a final thanks to the towboat. It was time to get moving. They had a long, hard passage before they reached Grand Bahama Island and the harbor at West End.

# SIX

THE REST OF THE TRIP THROUGH THE INTERCOASTAL waterway went smoothly. They passed under the very same viaduct they had crossed over earlier, and emerged in Port Everglades.

The lights on the ocean liners were still blazing. In the quiet of the night, the sound of music drifted across the water. The guests were up late, enjoying the food and entertainment. In the morning, they would be leaving port and making a quick trip to Nassau and Freeport.

In the harbor, there was no need to keep an eye on the depth gauge. Becca turned around in the cockpit and watched with fascination as they passed the giant ships. She felt as if she were riding in a toy.

"Look over there," Grandpa said, pointing to the far shore. "Can you see the submarines tied up next to the Coast Guard building?"

Becca could barely make out the sleek gray shapes. They seemed so mysterious, even menacing, in the light of the moon.

As they passed the subs, the open ocean came into view and the full force of the wind slammed into them. White capped waves broke over the bow, sending great streams of water washing over the deck. Grandpa once again hurried to the bow. It was time to raise the sails. They were about to leave the protection of the harbor.

"Check your heading," Grandpa called back to Grandma. The wind whipped the sound of his voice away.

"What?" Grandma yelled back.

"Your heading," he yelled again.

"Let's see the chart, Becca," Grandma said.

Becca held the chart flat and shined the flashlight on it. Grandma checked it, then leaned over and looked through the lighted compass mounted in front of her. She twisted and looked at the opening of the channel that was now lying behind them. She peered through the compass a second time and turned their bow slightly northward.

"We're going to be fighting to keep our head up," she called to Grandpa. "If the wind doesn't switch, we may have to change direction halfway and tack."

Grandpa didn't answer her. He was busy. The howling wind was fighting his efforts to raise the sails. The Diaspora's jib was coiled tightly against the front rigging.

Grandpa took a heavy stainless steel handle and fitted it into a winch. He pulled with both hands and slowly cranked up the jib. The wind filled the sail and the boat heeled over sharply. Becca put out her feet to keep from sliding off the seat and onto the floor of the cockpit. Grandma braced herself against the wheel and switched off the diesel engine.

Now Grandpa slowly and carefully inched his way amidships. He leaned inward and held onto the security bars running along the top of the pilot house. The waves broke over the side and soaked him to the skin. Becca watched fearfully.

The winch for the mainsail was located close to the cockpit. Grandpa slipped his arm through the security rail for support and began to crank the handle. The mainsail billowed out and the Diaspora leaped forward.

"George," Grandma yelled out. "We're doing almost eight knots. We'll have to reef in the mainsail."

"What?" he yelled back.

"We'll have to reef the sails to control our speed," Grandma repeated. "We're doing almost eight knots already."

There was an eerie whining sound coming from the rigging. The wires were bearing the extra strain of the gale force winds. The boat continued to heel on a severe angle and plunge through the heavy seas. First the bow would ride high up over the crest of a wave. Then it would drop suddenly into the following trough.

Grandpa reefed the mainsail to control their speed. He hauled back on a thick wire hanging from the boom. The sail puckered along its outer edge. That accomplished, he edged back to the cockpit.

"Here, I'll take over the wheel," he shouted above the wind when he finally reached them.

"You're going to change and get your storm gear on first," Grandma replied. "I'll be fine until you get back."

Grandpa didn't argue. Holding onto a railing for support, he pulled the hatch to the stairway half open and slid inside. He shut it tightly from below.

Becca curled her body into a corner of the cockpit. She didn't feel very secure. How could she, while the boat was leaning over and fighting the wind? The salt spray whipped against her face. It stung her eyes and left a thin, burning crust on her lips. She tried to think of this as an adventure, but fear crowded out any remnants of excitement.

"We're not in any danger?" she asked Grandma. "We won't break apart or sink, will we?"

Grandma forced a laugh. "No darling," she said. "We're only in danger of sore muscles. I'm sorry the weather had to be so bad. We've made this passage before and it's usually wonderful."

"Isn't this part of the Bermuda Triangle?" Becca asked. "Don't boats disappear here all the time?"

Her grandmother smiled grimly at her. "Don't worry Becca. I promised your mother I'd bring you home in one piece. Tomorrow, when we're moored at West End, this will seem like only a bad dream."

Grandpa slid open the hatch and pulled himself out. He was about to close it again, when he glanced over at Becca.

"You must be frozen," he said. "Go below and find the down jackets. They're in the locker with the life vests. Then put some rain gear on over it. Go on. You'll be warmer and much happier. Believe me."

Becca crawled over to the hatch. The boat was pitching so violently, she was afraid to stand up. Grandpa opened the doors and she lowered herself down the stairs.

Below deck, the rocking of the boat seemed even more severe. Becca tried to focus on the walls, the floor, anything to help her regain her feeling of security. Her head ached as if a band was being tightened across her forehead. She felt hot and flushed. Then her teeth began to chatter with cold. She reached out a hand to steady herself. The boat plunged sharply and her stomach seemed to push up against her lungs.

Now she knew what was wrong. She was seasick. She tried to swallow. Her throat was thick and unyielding. She tried to take a deep breath. The Diaspora rose and dropped again.

Ignoring the warm clothes hanging practically at her fingertips, Becca spun around and raced back up the stairs. Grandma saw her coming and reached out a hand to help. Becca missed her hand, slipped on the wet deck and crashed against the lazarette. She knelt on the seat, hung her head overboard and vomited.

Poor Becca. With each crashing plunge of the sailboat, her nausea increased. Her shoulders shook with the force of her retching stomach. Soon she had nothing left inside. She sank back into the cockpit.

"This isn't my idea of a vacation," Becca muttered weakly.

"It is an adventure though, isn't it?" Grandma said hopefully.

"Is it? Did I ask to have an adventure?"

"I remember you bragging about roller coaster rides," Grandpa called above the noise of the wind. "What ever happened to the girl who never gets sick?"

"Must have left her at home," Becca yelled back. "I'm not so sure this is adventure is worth the effort."

"Tell you what. Go get into dry gear and we'll talk."

"I'll help you," Grandma said. "I could use some dry clothes myself."

It didn't take long to change. They stripped off their wet things and dropped them into the shower. Grandma handed Becca a warm-up suit and took one for herself. Bright yellow, foul-weather gear pulled over their down jackets completed the change. At the last moment, Grandma grabbed the coffee thermos, plastic mugs and some granola bars.

Nothing had changed. The wind was still whistling through the rigging at 30 knots. The Diaspora was still plunging through heavy seas. The waves were still breaking over the bow and pouring down the deck.

Becca took a granola bar and wedged herself into the back corner of the cockpit. She was warm and dry. Her fear was finally under control. It had been replaced by a sense of wonder. For the first time in her life, she could truly appreciate the overwhelming force of nature. As the Diaspora struggled against wind and waves, Rebecca understood the awe of ancient people in the face of God's fury.

Beyond the boat's towering mast, Becca could catch glimpses of the moon. It shone through the ragged edges of the fast-moving clouds like a beacon. Its light flashed on the white, foaming crests of the waves.

Grandpa seemed to read her thoughts.

"It's as if we're making our own Exodus this night," he said suddenly. "It's not a weekend picnic in the park. It's the start of a journey to a distant land."

"I always thought of the Exodus as a happy event," Becca replied.

"Read your Tannach again," he said. "Moses had to listen to more griping than Ann Landers. Everything went wrong and everyone blamed him. First the Israelites hollered about the Egyptian soldiers. Then they complained about the lack of food. Then they blamed Moses for the lack of water.

"Even at Mount Sinai they complained. When he disappeared on the mountain for so long, they went and made the golden calf. Our Exodus from Egypt was one hardship after another. No question about it."

"It was worthwhile though," Grandma added. She was cradling a coffee cup close to her chest. She took a sip and handed it to Grandpa. He finished it in a single gulp.

"I like a difficult passage," Grandpa declared. "It keeps the adrenaline pumping."

"I'd like a warm bed," Becca replied. "It's three a.m. and I'm dead."

"Go to sleep," Grandma said. "There's nothing for you to do right now, anyway."

Becca sighed in relief. She blew a kiss to her grandparents and crawled over to the hatch.

Soon she was in her bunk, the warm quilt pulled over her head. The humming of the wires echoed inside the cabin and she could hear the crash of the waves hitting the bow right in front of her feet. She shuddered slightly, picturing towering walls of water tumbling movie-style all around. Exodus! The parting of the Red Sea! Even with that, exhaustion overtook her and she fell into a deep sleep.

# SEVEN

I T WAS NEARLY NOON WHEN BECCA AWOKE. SHE KNEW immediately that something was different. The dreadful jarring of the waves had stopped. The water passing along the bow had a pleasant gurgling sound. She sat up and peeked out her side porthole. The sky was clear and the ocean's surface was a gently rolling carpet of azure blue.

She hopped out of her bunk and went to the galley. Grandma was at the counter making sandwiches.

"Good morning, darling," she said to Becca. "How are you feeling now?"

"I'm fine Grandma. Only I'm really hungry. It's a good thing you're making lunch."

Becca carried the pitcher of lemonade and Grandma took care of the platter of sandwiches. They climbed up the stairs to the cockpit.

Grandpa was sitting on the back edge of the seat, holding the wheel steady with one bare foot. He looked calm, but very fatigued. His rain gear was lying in a heap on the cockpit floor.

"Well," he said. "How are the women folk doing? Are you rested and ready for duty?"

"I'm starved!" Becca told him.

"It's no wonder," he replied. "I seem to remember you feeding the fishes last night."

"I hope I never feel like that again," she said and reached for a sandwich.

Grandma took over the wheel. "Have something to eat, then you can get some rest," she told Grandpa. "Becca and I can handle the boat until we get to the rocks outside West End."

"Have you had enough sleep?" Grandpa asked. "You didn't go down until we were out of the gale."

"I was asleep by seven," she answered. "I'm fine...and we'll need your help going into the harbor."

They ate a leisurely lunch and enjoyed the sparkling sun. The rocking of the boat was comfortable, even reassuring. This was the way Becca had imagined her trip. She stretched out her long legs and let the sun soak in.

After lunch, she took charge of clearing the dishes. Grandma was busy at the helm and Grandpa went below, where he fell exhausted onto his bunk. Becca climbed down the steep stairs as quietly as possible. She felt good, knowing that she was actually helping. She didn't want to just go along for the ride. Finished at last, she went back on deck and dropped down on the lazarette next to Grandma.

"What happened last night while I was asleep?"

Grandma switched the boat onto auto-pilot and sat down next to Becca.

"Well, the wind kept howling for about another hour, so we just kept plowing along. Then, we got hit with a downpour that was totally blinding. That only lasted a few minutes, fortunately. Afterwards, the wind died away and finally switched to the south. That was around seven o'clock this morning."

"Did we have to change directions because of the storm? You said we might."

"We were lucky this time. The Gulf Stream is so powerful, that we were able to continue north-eastward without tacking. We're right on course and only a little bit behind schedule."

"What's going to happen now?" Becca asked.

"We should be able to continue like this until we reach West End. There are several small cays just outside the harbor. We'll have to be careful going past them. That's when we'll need Grandpa's help. We have to be right on target as we enter the marina. It's very shallow and we could get stuck again."

"Is that where we'll be having our seder?"

"That's right. It should be lots of fun."

"I'll bet we're the first Jews to ever celebrate Passover in the Bahamas," Becca declared.

"That's not a very safe bet," Grandma said. "West End is only a short distance from Freeport and the Luis de Torres Synagogue."

"There's a synagogue in the Bahamas?" Becca couldn't believe it.

"Oh my yes. Luis de Torres was Christopher Columbus' interpreter. It's quite likely that he was the first European to have stepped ashore in the New World. They landed at Samana Cay, right here in the Bahamas."

"And de Torres was Jewish?"

"Yes, but he was forced to convert to Catholicism in order to make the journey. Did you know that August 2, 1492 was the last day Jews were allowed to live in Spain? Columbus sailed the very next day."

"That's weird. I've never heard anything about it before."

"That's not the only coincidence. There's lots of evidence that Columbus' family had been Jewish, as well. His wife's family was. Some scholars believe he expected to find the lost tribes of Israel when he reached the Indies. Maybe that's why he brought along an interpreter who was fluent in Hebrew."

Becca giggled. "Poor guy. He didn't find India and he didn't find the lost Jewish tribes. Only Indian ones."

"De Torres ended up settling in these islands and began trading in tobacco. Soon after, many Spanish Jews fled to the Caribbean and started other new communities."

"I always thought of New York as the place for Jewish immigration. Is that wrong?"

"It's not wrong. It's just not the whole story. Jews have been living down here long before New York became important to our history."

"Where else did we settle?" Becca wondered.

"Jamaica. The Jewish community helped the British oust the Spaniards from that island in 1655. Their original synagogue was destroyed in an earthquake forty years later."

"Geez! That's a hundred years before the American Revolution."

"Right. Oh...I know a story relating to the Revolution, as a matter of fact. A large group of Dutch Jews were living on Saint Eustatius Island near the coast of Venezuela. They were supplying arms to the American colonies. The British weren't very happy about that and they leveled the city and deported everyone."

"Are there Jews on Saint Eustatius now?"

"No, but the oldest standing synagogue in the Western Hemisphere is on Curacao. That's part of the same group of islands, the Netherlands Antilles. It's the Mikve Israel-Emanuel, built in 1732. It's very beautiful."

"Does it look like our shul at home?"

"No. Not exactly. There are some differences."

"What kind of differences?"

"For one thing, most of the Caribbean synagogues have sand floors. That's a reminder of the days in Spain when Jews had to worship secretly in the basements of their homes. Still...there is a lot that's similar. Every shul has Torah scrolls and a ner tamid and a menorah. In fact, the menorah in the St. Thomas synagogue dates back to the days of Maimonides!"

Becca shook her head in disbelief. "I never knew any of this," she said. "To tell you the truth, Jewish history after the Maccabees is one big blur. How did you learn all these things?"

"I am always curious. That's the secret. You can't expect your teachers to give you everything. You have to keep learning on your own."

Becca stared up at the flags on the rigging. She thought of her upcoming Bat Mitzvah. She suddenly realized that it would mark the beginning of her religious education, not the end.

After a few minutes, she broke the silence.

"Would it be okay if I sunbathed on the the bow?"

"Go ahead, honey. Just don't lean over the railing. The boat can always take a sudden dip and I wouldn't want to have to fish you out of the ocean."

Becca glanced over the side at the frothing waves sweeping along the hull.

"How do you get someone back on board?" she asked.

Grandma pointed to the horseshoe buoy hooked nearby. "First we'd throw the buoy. Hopefully, you'd reach it, then we would have to come about and grab hold of you with the shepherd's crook. It's that pole belted to the rigging amidships."

Becca grimaced. "I think I'll be careful. Falling overboard doesn't seem like much fun."

Grandma nodded in agreement and went back to the wheel.

Becca stood up cautiously, but she discovered that walking along the deck was quite easy on this sunny afternoon. She thought about Grandpa fighting his way, inch by inch, struggling to reach the cockpit. It didn't seem real. It might have happened in a dream, many years ago. She lay with her head against the foreward hatch, closed her eyes and dozed off.

The time passed quickly. Almost before she knew it, Grandma called her back to the cockpit.

"Look out to the port side of the bow," she told Becca. "Do you see the two little cays at about ten o'clock?"

"Where's 10 o'clock?"

"Pretend the bowsprit is facing twelve o'clock and the stern is at six. Ten o'clock is on an angle to the left of the bow."

Becca stood up on the seat and shaded her eyes.

"I think I do," she said. "They look like two little lumps on the horizon."

"Yes," Grandma replied. "Here. Take a look through the binoculars."

Becca raised the binoculars to her eyes. The motion of the boat was also magnified and keeping the cays in sight was harder than she expected. Her legs felt very unsteady, so she dropped to her knees and rested her elbows on the back of the seat. Now she could sight in on the little islands. At this distance, they seemed barely more than large rocks clinging to the edge between water and sky.

"How long before we reach them?" she asked.

"Oh, I'd guess we'll be approaching the harbor within half an hour. We'll keep the cays on our port, then turn sharply when they are in a direct line with the piers in the marina. It's going to be a bit tricky and I'm afraid we'll be coming in after high tide."

"Do you think we'll get stuck again?" Becca asked.

"Well, I hope not," Grandma told her, "but nothing is ever certain. That's why sailing is always so exciting.

"Anyway," she continued, "you can wake up Grandpa soon. I'll need him, plus any help we can get from the people on the dock."

"I'd like to help too," Becca said. "There must be something I can do."

"Sometimes I can't hear what your grandfather is yelling," Grandma said thoughtfully. "If you would stand amidships and relay all his instructions, that would be a big help."

"Sure. I can do that. But isn't there anything else? I would like to do something really important."

Grandma smiled at her. "Getting the instructions right is just about the most important job on the boat," she said. "If you really want to, though, you could throw out one of the spring lines, as well."

"Oh yes!" Becca said. She paused, then asked. "How would I do that?"

"Well, sometimes the dockmaster is on hand to catch the lines and secure them. Sometimes Grandpa has to jump off quickly and do it himself. Just throw your line to whomever. West End is a nice size harbor. I'm sure there will be plenty of people around to help."

As they talked, the Diaspora made steady progress toward Grand Bahama Island. It lay low, hugging the whole horizon. The two rocky cays stood like guards across from the curved peninsula sheltering the harbor.

Becca picked up the binoculars again. Now she could see the spiky outline of trees on the big island. She lowered the glasses and looked at the navigational charts. Grand Bahama seemed to fill up the entire ocean.

Next, she flipped to the world atlas at the front of the packet. It showed the east coast of the United States, the whole Atlantic ocean and the shoreline of Europe and Africa.

Where was Grand Bahama Island? For that matter, where were the Bahamas in general? Becca bent down to get a closer look. The entire nation, all seven hundred islands of the Bahamas, was represented by a few dots off the coast of Florida. It seemed miraculous that they had traveled all night and day, out of the sight of land, and were now coming in directly on course.

Grandma seemed to read her mind. "Amazing isn't it. I always think about the explorers taking off across the ocean. It seems impossible that any of them survived. Then they made it home again, as well. It's crazy...we need our charts and radar and depth finders, just to make this little trip from Florida."

Becca laughed. "That's what I was thinking. How did Columbus ever make it here? What kept him from sailing around in circles? There's nothing to see in the middle of the ocean."

"Oh, they weren't completely helpless. They knew the positions of the stars. They had astronomical tables and some other instruments. When you get a chance, ask Grandpa to explain how a Jacob's Staff works.

"Speaking of Grandpa, could you go down and wake him? I'm going to need his guidance very soon."

Becca slipped quickly down the stairs into the salon. The door to Grandpa's cabin was open. She stepped in and tapped him on the shoulder.

"What's wrong?" he asked as he sprang from his bed.

"Everything's fine," she told him. "We're almost at West End."

Grandpa checked his watch. "Seventeen hundred hours," he muttered. "I hope we'll get into the harbor on time."

As soon as he got on deck, he picked up the binoculars and carefully scanned the horizon. Then he looked at the navigational charts and took a sighting of the harbor entrance with the compass.

"That's very good, Maggie," he said. "You've got us right where we belong. We won't have any trouble with the outside cays. What's our knot reading, Becca?"

Becca searched the instrument panel. She found the knot indicator to the left of the depth gauge.

"It says three knots," she reported.

"Hmmmmm," Grandpa muttered. "Too slow. I'd like to get there faster."

"Are you worried about the tide," Becca asked him.

"See! I told you she wasn't so dumb!" he said to Grandma with a smile. "She might grow up to be a useless, I mean useful, person after all."

He winked at Becca, then asked her. "What do you think we should do?"

Becca studied the sails. Grandpa had put out all three of them after the storm passed. No more to do there. They were on the right course, so changing directions wouldn't help. She scratched the back of her head. Suddenly, the answer came to her.

"Why don't we turn the motor back on."

"Right on, Kiddo. Grandma, start the engine."

The diesel coughed momentarily, then came to life. The boat vibrated under their feet and the knot meter swung up to five.

"I've got a question Grandpa," Becca said.

"So ask."

"Grandma said I should ask you how a Jacob's Staff works. Could you explain it?"

"Ah...You were talking about Colombus, I suppose."

"I was wondering how he ever got here?"

"You know, there's some talk that he may have been a Marrano, a converted Jew. He used to brag that he was related to King David."

"King David!"

"Yeah. And before he became the great admiral, he was an expert map-maker. At that time in history, almost all the cartographers were Spanish Jews."

"That's very curious."

"I certainly think so. Whatever the explanation, we do know that most of his friends were Jews. He relied on Jewish mathematicians and astronomers for his information."

"His interpretation too," Becca added.

"Right. Now, early navigation was celestial. Everything related to the position of the stars or the sun. Columbus sailed with Abraham Zacuto's astronomical tables. He needed to know the position of the stars on each day of the year. Zacuto's information was the best."

"What about the Jacob's Staff?"

"It was an instrument for determining latitude, how far north or south of the equator you were. The Portuguese Scientific Committee developed it. And almost everyone on the committee was Jewish. You have to wonder why, even though he wasn't sailing for Portugal, they still gave it to Columbus."

"How important was it?"

"With it, he could estimate his latitude by measuring the angle between the horizon and the sun at noon. Without it, he probably would not have been able to return to Spain. He wouldn't have known where it was."

Becca felt a little tingle of excitement. It was as if she were a detective, discovering new and important facts. She had never realized how important Jewish history was to the rest of the world.

It had always seemed like some minor footnote, learned at shul and then forgotten.

A light spray of salt water drew her attention back to the present. The increased speed from the diesel was churning up the waves as they passed through. She leaned out to see the cays more clearly.

The top of the rocks were white with a constantly moving mass of seagulls. The sides of the rocks were streaked with droppings. Becca could see the waves breaking against the cays. With each big breaker, the crowd of birds rose into the air screaming with delight. Becca thought they looked like the screaming people on the water rides at the fair.

The entrance to the harbor was hidden from her, so she decided to walk out to the bow.

"Can I stand on the bowsprit?" she asked.

"Only if you promise to be extra careful," Grandma replied.

"Oh, I will," Becca promised. "I'll hold onto the ropes the entire time."

"Okay," Grandpa said, "but you'll have to change places with me just as soon as we start into port. I have to help guide us in."

Becca climbed out of the cockpit and made her way up to the very front of the boat. The bowsprit stuck out another four feet. It was only eighteen inches across, with wide spaces between narrow boards. Becca looked down and could see the water rushing all foamy white below her feet.

The wind came rushing around her body. She felt encased by its strong embrace. Her long brown hair streamed back and her earrings tugged to get loose. Becca felt totally free. She laughed out loud. Almost as if in answer, the seagulls on the rocks rose and screamed in unison.

# EIGHT

NTERING THE HARBOR WAS A PIECE OF CAKE. THEIR sails were down and they motored in cautiously past the other yachts tied up at the marina. For one brief moment, the Diaspora brushed the sandy bottom, but Grandma pushed up the throttle ever so slightly and they slid right over it.

Grandma swung the boat wide around the end of the pier. Then she brought them to a stop by shifting into reverse. When the momentum of the big boat ceased, she shifted forward once more and eased the bow slowly into their slip. It was as smooth as a compact car parking in the family garage.

Grandpa threw the bowline to the waiting dock master, who quickly tied it to a big solid post.

"Your turn, Becca," Grandpa shouted to her. Becca took her tightly coiled line and tossed it out carefully. The man tied it to a post near the Diaspora's bow. Then he took a line from Grandpa and fastened it to a huge cleat bolted to the pier at the stern. The interaction of these spring lines, crossing each other the full length of the boat, held them steady in the berth.

"Well done crew," Grandpa said to Becca as he came back to the cockpit. "Beautiful job, Captain," he said to Grandma.

"I had to do it perfectly this time," she replied. "After smacking into that charter boat last night, I felt I had to redeem myself."

Grandpa gave her a big bear hug and a kiss. "I've already forgotten about last night. This trip is going to be great fun. We promised the little girl, what's her name, that she would enjoy herself.

"Are you enjoying yourself?" he asked Becca. "Better say yes!"

"Yes, yes, yes," Becca told him. "But I hope I don't throw up anymore. I didn't like that part so much."

"Diaspora," the dock master called out. "I have to fill in my report. You are flying the yellow Quarantine flag. Is this your first port of call?"

"Yes," Grandpa replied. "We'll go and clear customs and immigration right away. Is the government office still on the beach?"

"Yes, Captain," the darkly tanned young man replied. "Right over there at the picnic tables. I'll call immigration for you."

Grandpa shaded his eyes with his hand and looked towards the shore.

As soon as the dock master left, the three of them went below deck to gather their papers. Grandpa took their boat registration and passports out of the safe. Becca dug her official, notarized birth certificate out of the drawer.

"I'm very thirsty," Grandma said as they met back in the salon. "I think I'll bring along a pitcher of lemonade. Do you think there will be any objection if I do?"

"What's the worse thing that could happen?" Grandpa asked her. "Maybe we'll have to share it with the customs inspector."

The Passover Passage 67

Becca giggled and Grandpa pinched her cheek. "Personally, I'd be more worried about this unidentified child who snuck on board. I think we'll have to leave her behind."

"Stop it Grandpa," Becca protested. "I'm not unidentified. I've got my birth certificate. See. It even has a little gold seal on it, to show it's official."

"Does this mean we're stuck with her?" he asked Grandma, pretending to be greatly alarmed.

"You're stuck with me," Becca declared.

"Drat!" he growled. "Well, let's not keep the inspector waiting."

Off to the beach they marched. They settled down at the first table under the trees. The sun filtered through the fronds of the palms. The boats stood out in stark contrast to the clear blue water. It looked like a scene from a postcard. Grandma poured lemonade and they waited to clear customs.

The minutes ticked away. They were on their second glassful, when a battered truck pulled up. A small man carrying a big, old leather briefcase approached them.

"Are you the Diaspora?" he asked. He pronounced it like "Diaz Poura."

"Yes," Grandpa replied.

"I'm sorry Captain," he said. "You are not sitting at the proper table for customs inspections. I will have to ask you to move."

They looked at him with surprise. There were only three tables on the beach.

"Where should we be?" Grandma asked politely.

"My table is the last one on the left, madam," the small man replied. "If you would kindly transfer to that location, I can begin."

Grandpa shrugged and picked up the folder with his documents. Grandma picked up the pitcher and the cups. Becca followed behind, clutching her certificate and hoping that it would be adequate.

Once they had reported to the proper table, the inspection took very little time. The man scanned the documents. He stamped Grandma and Grandpa's passports and smiled at Becca.

"So, young woman. Is this your first trip to our islands?"

"Yes, sir," she replied.

"You are sailing all around with your grandparents?"

She nodded.

"Our islands are most beautiful. You will want to come back often." He smiled at her and closed up his briefcase.

"Captain," he said. "You are no longer quarantined. You may remove the yellow flag. Do you have a Bahamian flag?"

"Certainly," Grandpa replied. "I will raise a courtesy flag immediately."

"You may fly it until you leave Bahamian waters. You will not have to clear customs again." He handed a card to Grandpa. "When you return home, mail this card to us."

"Thank you," Grandpa said.

The man nodded pleasantly. "Have a nice stay," he said and walked back to his waiting truck.

It was early evening by this time. The sun was low in the sky. It seemed huge, hovering over the mouth of the harbor. The wind had died completely and everything seemed hushed.

Back on the Diaspora, Becca and her grandparents lounged in the cockpit and ate their dinner. Grandma hadn't fussed. She threw together a salad and some rolls. The strain of the night passage was telling on them. Grandpa put his plate on the floor and stretched out on his back. In a minute, he had fallen asleep.

"What are we going to do now?" Becca whispered.

"Your Grandpa's going to sleep," Grandma replied.

"I can see that. But what can we do?"

Grandma groaned. She was tired too. Then she smiled. "I could stretch my legs. We've been sitting for almost twenty hours. Tell you what. I'll throw the dishes in the sink and we can go for a walk."

As the sky grew dark, Becca and Grandma walked together along the beach. They passed a pretty hotel sitting by the ocean. During the daytime, the Bahamian women sold their fruits and vegetables and little straw dolls under the tall palm trees that lined the shore.

"Tomorrow, we'll come back and buy some fresh fish for our seder," Grandma said. "One of the nicest young fishermen in all the islands lives here. Your grandpa always takes some time to talk with him. He can count on Josef to give us accurate information on the bottom conditions."

"I thought you had charts for that."

"We do, but the bottom is sandy and shifts with the tides and the storms. Generally, we play it safe and figure that areas are shallower than the charts indicate. When we get good local information, it helps a great deal."

They had to step carefully to avoid tripping over stones and branches in the dark. The water in the harbor picked up eerie flashes of color, deep rich blue and rose and liquid gold.

The cabin lights were on in the Diaspora. Grandpa had awakened from his nap and was working at his nav station.

"Hi girls," he said without looking up. "Where have you been?"

"Keeping out of your way, dear," Grandma told him.

"We walked around the beach, past the hotel. We went as far as the market tables in the palm tree grove," Becca added.

She walked to the desk and peeked over his shoulder. He was comparing two sets of charts of Grand Bahama and the surrounding Abaco islands.

"Grandma said you get updated information from someone here at West End."

"That's true, but reviewing the charts beforehand helps me to visualize the areas as Josef tells me about them. You can never be too prepared," Grandpa replied.

"Can I help you plan our course to the next island?"

"I don't see why not, but it's a bit too soon to worry about that. Anyway, it's bedtime. Go on and get out of here."

Becca kissed both of them goodnight and headed for her cabin. The blackness of the night pressed in all around the boat. She was very tired and ready for sleep.

# NINE

THE NOISY CHATTER OF BIRDS WOKE BECCA EARLY the next morning. Through the hatch over her head, she could see the brilliant blue sky. The flags hung limply on the rigging. She stretched lazily under the light quilt and closed her eyes again. No need to get up early this morning.

Suddenly, a cascade of water splashed down the side of the boat right next to her. She bolted upright, hitting her head on the little reading light.

"Ouch!" she yelled.

Grandpa stuck his head down the hatch.

"You always holler when you wake up?"

"I hit my head. What are you doing? It's so early."

"I'm cleaning the brass. A couple of days in the salt spray and it turns all green. Of course, I'm not sure why I'm doing it. I thought that's why you're aboard."

"I thought vacations were for relaxing."

"You relaxed all night. My gosh, what a lazy crew I've got. That lady I married is still sleeping, too."

"Guess again," Grandma called from the galley.

Becca leaned out of the bunk and stuck her head around the cabin door.

"Good morning, darling," Grandma said and kissed her forehead. "Tell your grandfather that breakfast will be ready in a few minutes. He should hurry up with the brass."

Becca stood up and wiggled her head and shoulders out of the hatch. "Grandma says breakfast will be ready in a few minutes."

"No problem," Grandpa told her. "Put your bathing suit on. It's gorgeous out here."

Becca hopped out of bed and yanked on her drawer. It would not budge. She tried jiggling it, then she tried hitting it with her fist. It still would not budge.

"Help! My clothes are being help prisoner."

Grandma finished pouring the steaming coffee into the thermos and pushed it aside.

"Now what seems to be the problem?" she asked.

"I give up with this stupid drawer," Becca told her. "Half the time, I can't get it open and the other half I can't get it shut."

Grandma eyed the stubborn drawer carefully. "The left corner is down somewhat," she said. "Here watch. I'll lift the drawer up on an angle to even out the two sides. Now, you see the drawer slides open." She grunted softly as she tugged.

"I'll never get it," Becca lamented. "I feel so dumb asking for help opening a drawer."

"Forget it," Grandma said. "Come on. Get dressed. We'll eat breakfast on the deck."

They ate slowly and leisurely, relaxing in the hot morning sun. Becca took one last bite out of her sweet roll. She licked her fingers, leaned over the side of the boat and dropped the crumbs from her plate into the water.

"YEOW!" she yelped and nearly dropped the plate overboard, too.

She had thought a few curious fish might swim over and investigate the crumbs. Instead, two sleek grey creatures flashed out from below the boat. They struck at the falling morsels, almost before they hit the water.

Grandpa was at her side in an instant.

"What's the matter?"

"They're gone already," Becca said. "Two grey fish. They looked like miniature sharks. I threw some of my sweet roll overboard and they raced out from under the boat. I guess I wasn't expecting them."

"Could have been nurse sharks," Grandma said.

"Or barracuda," Grandpa added.

"But they were real small."

"So? They could have been babies," Grandpa replied.

"Is it safe to swim around here? I mean, if there are sharks and barracudas around?"

"Sure, it's safe," Grandpa winked at her. "You don't look like a raspberry sweet roll to me."

"Grandpa!" Becca said impatiently. "I'm serious. I want to go swimming, but I don't want to end up eaten by sharks."

"You don't have to worry, dear," Grandma assured her.

"That's right Rebecca," Grandpa said seriously. "You're too big for a couple of baby whatevers to munch on."

"Thanks alot. Am I supposed to feel better now?"

"You worry too much. We'll go together to the beach. I'm reasonably sure we'll come back in one piece."

"Well, okay. When can we go? It's incredibly hot this morning."

"In a minute," Grandpa said. He lifted the pad off the bench and began digging in the lazarette. "I just remembered something I stuck in here, before we left Key Largo."

Grandpa straightened up and held out a black bag with a long hose attached to it.

"What in the world is that?" Becca asked.

"It's a solar shower," he replied. "After you swim in the ocean, you'll want to wash off the salt. Rather than use the generator to produce hot water, we can use the sun. I'll fill this bag with fresh water, then hang it from the rigging. By the time we finish swimming, it should be nice and warm."

"I saw one of those at the camping store back home. Does it really work?"

"We'll see, won't we." He carried the contraption to the bow of the Diaspora and hooked it to the jib lines.

"Hop onto the dock," he told Becca, "and hand the fresh water hose up here."

Becca jumped over to the pier and wrestled the thick black hose over to the side of the boat. Grandpa reached through the railing and snaked it on board.

"Turn it on," he called when he had attached it to the bag.

Becca pulled the lever on the water supply and the solar shower ballooned.

"Enough!" Grandpa yelled. Becca turned it off quickly.

"Now we'll hoist it up into the sunshine, and go off for our swim.

"Maggie!" he called. "Let's get going!"

Grandma emerged from the boat with a big woven bag slung over her shoulder.

"I've got sunscreen for everyone," she said. "We're not going anywhere until we're covered. Especially you," she scolded her husband. "The doctor said he's removed too many patches of skin cancer from you already!"

The walk to the beach would have taken less than five minutes, if they hadn't stopped to shop at the tables under the big palm trees. This morning they were loaded with goods. Crowds of people wandered about. Women wearing flowered cotton dresses and straw hats, sat contentedly on folding chairs, gossiping with their neighbors. Little children played beneath the tables. The older children were the salesmen.

Grandma stopped and bought three small, but fragrant oranges from one table. A little further down, she picked out a woven hat and plunked it on Becca's head.

"Now you look like a native," she said.

Becca removed the hat and examined it. The fronds were still green and plump. It had a pleasant odor.

"Do I look like a yutz?" she asked as she put it back on her head.

"Definitely," Grandpa answered. "I'd get it, if I were you."

"Sold," she said, and Grandma paid the woman with a brightly colored Bahamian bill.

At the end of the row, there was a tall, slender boy of fifteen. He stood, net in hand, next to a galvanized washtub filled with swimming fish.

"There's our friend," Grandma said to Becca.

Becca felt oddly attracted to him. He was, she observed, rather handsome, with skin the color of carmel. His shaggy, wind-tossed hair was dark brown, tinged with sunbleached strands.

The boy met her gaze with a look of curiosity. His light grey eyes stared into hers. She blushed and turned to look at the ocean.

Grandma noticed the unspoken exchange, but politely ignored it.

"Good morning, Josef,' she said. "How have you and your family been?"

"We have been well over these many months, Madame Captain," he replied. "It has been with great anticipation I have waited for your return. And then, yesterday, I saw the Diaspora glide into the harbor. All night, I watched the anchor light on top of her golden mast. It shone like a star. I could barely sleep, looking at that light. I kept dreaming about distant lands and my heart sounded as loud as a drum."

Becca turned back and looked at the boy in amazement. His words sounded like poetry. She thought it strange that a ragged, barefoot native would speak with such elegance.

His eyes darted quickly to her own. This time she didn't turn away, but returned his stare.

Grandpa wrapped an arm around the boy's shoulders.

"We'll be in port a few days," he said. "Come down to the marina when you're free and we'll discuss the charts."

Josef nodded, then asked, "Who is your lovely companion?"

"Oh, I'm sorry," Grandma said. "This is our granddaughter Becca. That's short for Rebecca. Becca Able, meet Josef Albury."

Josef took Becca's hand in both of his.

"It is the greatest pleasure for me to meet you," Josef said. "You are a most fortunate young woman. Your grandparents are very kind people."

Becca blushed a fiery red. She could only nod in reply.

"Say something, you dope," she thought to herself. "He's going to think you're a totally social reject."

Grandma rescued her.

"We're on our way to the beach for a swim," she interjected quickly. "But when we're done, we're going to need a nice fish for dinner.

She poked her hand into the water.

"What do you think, George?" Grandma asked.

"Looks like the Yellowtail is the right size," he replied.

"I thought so too."

Becca finally found her voice.

"We'll be back after we swim," she said to Josef. "Don't sell that fish to anyone else. Okay?"

"I'll be here, waiting for you to return."

Becca smiled slightly and looked over at Grandma. Grandma's eyebrows lifted in a silent question, but Becca put on a look of cool indifference.

"Let's go swimming," she said to her grandparents. "I'm dying from sunstroke."

Down the beach, the cool aqua water sparkled in the sun. The smooth bottom was clearly visible far out from the shore.

"I'll meet you," Becca called over her shoulder and ran across the sand.

The clarity of the water was deceptive. Becca took a running leap into the surf and found herself being tumbled head over heels. Instead of six inches, she found herself in six feet of water. She opened her eyes in surprise, forgetting that she was swimming in salt water. With stinging eyes and empty lungs, she burst up to the surface.

The undertow had pulled her away from the shore. For a brief moment, she panicked. Then she forced herself to relax. She stretched out on a wave and body-surfed back to the beach.

Grandpa waded out to the rescue. Becca reached for his hand and he grabbed her.

"Hey Maggie!" he yelled. "I caught a fish. Don't bother buying that other one. This one's even bigger." Becca laughed and tried to dunk his head.

"Help me Grandma," she yelled. "I've got to drown this octopus. It's got me. Help!"

Grandma floated by on one of the air mattresses she had packed in her bag.

"While you two drown each other, I'm going to float around and enjoy the sun."

"May I have a mat?" Becca asked. The idea of floating around in the quiet bay seemed like heaven.

"Only if you blow up one for me," Grandpa said.

Becca waded ashore and took the two deflated mattresses from Grandma's bag. She sat on the sand and blew them up. Then, hot and tired from the effort, she splashed back into the ocean.

No one said much after that. Somehow, being together was enough. The hot, strong sun beat down on them. The clear water cooled them. Becca closed her eyes and the image of Josef's face filled her mind. She heard the soft cadence of his voice.

"It's so strange," she thought to herself, "I've always thought of the islands as a distant and exotic land. He looks out at the ocean and thinks of America the very same way."

She squeezed her eyes tight, trying to erase his image. Everything faded, except his light grey eyes. They stared at her unflinchingly. At first she felt flushed, then she began to feel silly.

"Go away," she mumbled.

"B-CAW," came the answer.

Her eyes flew open in surprise. Right next to her face, a seagull was floating placidly on the water.

"B-CAW," she answered back.

The gull stretched out its wings and dipped its head under the water. Becca tried to sneak her hand out to touch its back, but it rose into the air with one more loud, and this time indignant, call.

Grandma opened her eyes and looked at her watch.

"We've been in over an hour," she said. "I would hate for us to end up sunburned. Time to head back to the boat. We can try out our new shower."

"Do you think the water will be warm yet?" Becca asked.

"Could be," Grandpa replied. "I think Grandma's right. We should get out of the water before we fall asleep and float out to sea."

They paddled to shore and gathered their belongings. As they walked the short distance back to the palm grove, Becca could feel the boy watching them. Soon, she could see him; his feet planted firmly in the sand; his hand shielding his eyes from the sun.

"There's our good fellow," Grandpa said clapping him on the shoulder. "Still have that Yellowtail for us?"

"I would never fail to keep a promise to my friends," Josef replied, as he pulled the fish from the tub. With a quick slash, he cut off the head and cleaned out the entrails. He wrapped it in newspaper and handed it to Grandpa.

"This is a very large fish for only three people," he said. "In my home, it would feed twice as many."

Grandma laughed and replied with a touch of embarrassment, "Americans do tend to overeat, I know. This fish is for a celebration, however. Tonight is a holiday."

The boy tilted his head. "A holiday at night? I know nothing of this holiday."

"Tonight we remember the exodus from Egypt."

"Oh yes. I have heard of this. It was the last supper of Jesus. You follow the customs of the Old Testament."

"There's nothing old about it," Becca exclaimed, unexpectedly. She surprised herself, and stepped back, confused by her strong emotions. She wanted him to understand. It seemed terribly important.

Josef stared into her eyes once again. He began to speak, but then hesitated.

"Leaving a land of captivity is something to celebrate," he said quietly. "I will be thinking of your happiness this evening."

"Would you like to join us?" Grandma asked quickly. "Passover is a time for sharing with others."

Becca looked at him hopefully.

The boy shook his head. "It is not my celebration," he sighed. Hands hanging loosely at his side, he walked away from them. He stood at the water's edge and gazed out to the horizon.

# TEN

**B**ACK AT THE BOAT, GRANDPA RINSED THE FISH, then stored it in the refrigerator. He grabbed a bar of soap and joined the women, who were waiting on the bow.

"This was your idea originally," he said to Grandma, "so you get the first turn."

He took the nozzle and pushed the release button. Hot water sprinkled out. He held it high and each of them enjoyed the pleasure of a hot, fresh-water shower. Becca twirled around and around under the thin stream. It felt good to wash away the coating of salt that had dried on her skin.

After a quick lunch, it was time to begin preparing for the seder.

Grandma and Becca left Grandpa topside. He was busy shining brass and rinsing the teakwood deck. They sat down at the salon table to plan their meal.

"Let's discuss the seder plate first," Grandma said. "What will we need?"

"Parsley and salt water," Becca said.

"Check."

"Moror."

"We bought horseradish in Florida. Check."

"Charoset."

"We have apples, nuts and wine. You get to make that," Grandma said.

"Hard-boiled egg."

"We have eggs. We'll boil a few."

"We don't have a shank bone, Grandma."

"Ah ha!" she answered. "I planned ahead for that. We had lamb some time back, while we were in Florida. The shank bone's in our freezer."

"Then there's matzah, of course. And I know we have that."

"Okay," Grandma said and wrote on her notepad. "Rebecca makes charoset. Grandma boils eggs. Now, how about our dinner?"

"Grandma Ida always starts with gefilte fish."

"Your grandfather's not too fond of gefilte fish."

"It wouldn't seem like Pesach without it. I know how to make it. I help Grandma with it every year."

"We'd need another fish."

"I'd be happy to go back and get one."

Grandma winked at her. "I imagine so," she laughed.

"Grandma!"

"He's a very nice youngster and he seemed to like you, too."

"Stop it, Grandma. I don't like to be laughed at."

"I'm not laughing, sweetheart. Go ahead and get your fish. I'll work on the soup while you're gone."

Becca started toward the stairs, then hesitated. Her emotions were all mixed up. Did she want to return, by herself, to the palm grove? Maybe not. She turned back to the galley. She needed time to sort out her feelings.

"I know we have matzah meal for knaidlach," she said, "but how are you going to make the soup?"

"Through the magic of instant dried soup mix," Grandma replied. "We'll put in some carrots and onions. It will be almost as good as homemade. Now, let's think about the logistics for this situation. We'll have to boil the matzah balls, the soup and the gefilte fish in separate pots. I hope the galley doesn't get too hot."

"How can it get any hotter than it is already? I'm sweating in my bathing suit. I suppose we'll also have to light the oven for the fish."

"No need. I'll cover it with lemon slices, wrap it in clear plastic and microwave it to tender perfection. We can serve a fresh fruit platter and green salad to go with it."

"What about dessert?"

"Unfortunately, I can't make my famous matzah meal, nut cake. It would be an awful mess in this little galley. However, someone did bring aboard chocolate swirl ice cream. I think that should do the trick."

"I forgot all about it!"

"I know you did. Grandpa did too. Good thing, otherwise there wouldn't be any left for our dessert tonight. You know, if you're serious about the extra fish, you have to go get it now."

"I've been thinking about it. It really seems like too much work," Becca replied. She tried to sound cool and reserved, but she felt uncomfortable and flustered.

"I am so dumb," she thought to herself. "What's my problem? We're leaving West End in a day or two. I'll never see him again."

"I guess I'll just stay here and help you," she finished weakly.

Grandma and Becca set to work on their holiday meal. While three eggs boiled on the top of the little stove, Grandma stirred two other eggs into the matzah meal. She added oil and a little water, then put the bowl into the refrigerator. She bumped into Rebecca as she bent down. Becca bumped her back.

"You forgot the salt, Grandma," she scolded.

"No. I left out the salt. The seasonings in the broth will be enough. Your grandfather doesn't need any more."

"He's going to complain."

"He'll never notice. Say, how are you doing on the apple chopping?"

"Okay. Do you think one apple's really enough?"

"There's only three of us. Besides, we like it heavy on nuts."

Becca popped a walnut into her mouth and chewed it thoughtfully.

"I like nuts too. I always have to make a bowl of charoset without nuts, just apples, grape juice and honey for the little kids. Guess that's not a problem tonight."

"We don't have grape juice. I hope you won't mind the wine."

"Could I drink some wine tonight?"

"You could taste some, I suppose. You're not driving afterward, are you?"

"Grandma!"

"I didn't think so. Okay, let's stop eating all the nuts and put this bowl in the fridge. We have the rest of the fruit and salad vegetables to clean."

While they were cleaning the produce, they heard Grandpa talking to someone up on deck. Becca strained to hear the other voice, but the rumble of the generator drowned it out.

Before long, they could hear a light thud as someone jumped on board. Immediately afterwards, Grandpa climbed down the stairs. Josef was with him.

"I invited Josef to see the radar equipment," Grandpa explained.

"All done selling for today?" Grandma asked.

"Yes M'am. All my fish have been sold. I hope you don't mind that I came to visit at this time."

"We're always happy to have you on board"

Becca fought off a wave of shyness. "I like to study family histories," she said to him. "Where does your last name, Albury, come from?"

"It's English," he replied. "It is one of the most common names in the Islands. My father's family came here during your Revolutionary War. They were British loyalists, who left Virginia. My mother's family were Spanish pirates and African slaves. I'm a mix of all peoples." He swept his hand from his head downward.

"I like that," Grandpa said. "Alburys and Ables. Kind of cozy. Come on over here, young man. I'll show you the radar."

The boat suddenly seemed much smaller as all four of them crowded amidship. Becca put down her paring knife and squeezed over towards the radar scope. It was set in the wall across from the microwave oven.

Grandpa turned on the radar. The scope glowed green and began to make the characteristic "whoosh" sound of the tracking beam. Faint outlines of the shore and nearby boats formed.

"We're looking at the closest radius," Grandpa explained. "Think of it like the concentric rings formed when you throw a pebble in the water. By dialing this knob," he said turning it in his fingertips, "you can focus on whatever radius you want. See? Now we're looking at the cays outside the harbor."

Josef stepped forward and pressed his forehead against the rubber viewing collar. He played with the different distance readings and then stepped back.

"That's wonderful," he sighed. "I would like to know how all of these instruments work." He waved his hand at the radar, the Loran, the satellite weather readout, the VHF receivers. "There's so much to learn about, but I'll never be anything except a fisherman."

"There are always books," Grandpa said. "Even when you're finished with school, you can go to the library."

Josef laughed ruefully. "Have you seen the library at West End? It is a tiny place, with books so old, no one else wants them. If I read every book there, I'd still be thirty years behind."

"What about Freeport?" Grandma asked.

"There is no money to go to Freeport. And even in Freeport, I would not be able to truly keep up with the newest technology."

"You could come to America with us!" Becca blurted out.

Josef's grey eyes looked cloudy with a deep pain.

"Some things can only be dreams," he said.

There was a long pause as they each searched their minds and hearts for an answer.

"Join us for dinner," Grandpa said at last. "After we read the Haggadah, the story of Passover, we can talk. We are a people who believe in the possibilities of dreams."

Josef rubbed his chin thoughtfully and gazed around the boat. His eyes drank in every detail.

"It's been a year since I last went to school," he said quietly. "I completed only eight grades, although I was the best student in my whole school. There were twenty of us."

"Will you join our seder?" Grandma asked.

"If my parents allow it," he replied, "then I will return."

"Seven o'clock," Grandma said. "We begin at sundown. I hope you'll come back."

"Seven," Josef repeated. "I would like that also."

He shook Grandpa's hand and left the boat.

"Interesting problem," Grandpa said, breaking the silence that followed. He walked into the salon and took the Haggadot from their drawer below the bookshelf. They were ragged and wine splashed. Some of the pictures had been colored with crayons.

"Good thing I brought my Haggadah," Becca observed. "Yours are falling apart. Should Dad send you new ones for next year?"

"Absolutely not," he replied. "These are precious heirlooms. Come look at the inside covers."

Inside each Haggadah were handwritten columns of family memories. At the head of each column, there was a date. Next came a listing of family members present. There were notations on the whereabouts of missing individuals. Comments about funny incidents that had occurred during the meal. There were notations written by her great grandfather. There were scribbles made by her Dad when he was only two. It was a family chronicle that reached back thirty years.

Becca read it over. "Here I am, " she said. "First grandchild, Rebecca, asleep upstairs. I must have been two months old."

"When dinner was over," Grandma recalled, "We laid you on the table and everyone admired you."

Becca blushed slightly. Then she said, "Here's something interesting. A very old entry, '3 baby boys asleep in next room' and exactly twenty-five years later, "3 baby boys asleep in next room.'"

"Your uncle and his two cousins," Grandpa explained. "Then your brother Alex and his two cousins."

Becca read on.

"Oh no! Did the dog really throw up on Grandpa Jake's foot?"

"During seder," Grandma said nodding. "We had to stop and clean up under the table. That silly animal was not invited to any more Passover dinners."

Becca read through every entry. The torn, stained booklets were testimony to the dedication of generations past and present. She looked forward to adding her own entry for this night.

# ELEVEN

A cool breeze sprang up as the sun approached the horizon. The harbor was filled with the liquid gold reflection of the sky. They had changed their clothes and were sitting on deck. Waiting. As the last sliver of the sun disappeared into the ocean, Josef walked up the pier to the Diaspora. The light of early evening gave his skin a glow. His hair was neatly combed back; his tee-shirt replaced by a smoothly ironed, white dress shirt.

"Shalom," Grandpa said, as he helped him on board.

"Thank you for sharing our celebration," Grandma added.

"I return to your company with pleasure." He looked directly at Becca. She felt shivery under his gaze. Her stomach felt tight and it seemed difficult to breath. She ducked her chin to avoid his eyes.

"It's time to begin, children," Grandma said quickly. "Let's go inside."

At the dining table, Grandpa ceremoniously entered a new column into the cover of his Haggadah. Becca opened hers and made a notation.

"My first annual Passover diary," she said.

"Now even your great-grandchildren will know that you celebrated Pesach in West End," Grandpa told her. "They can read about this night. They'll know that their ancient ancestors...that's you and me Maggie...were with you. They'll discover that we shared our seder with our friend Josef. This is a special night for all of us."

"Becca looked at her wobbly handwriting. "Something this significant should look better," she laughed.

"Here. Allow me," Josef said.

He took the Haggadah from her. With a beautiful flourish he wrote "JOSEF ALBURY DINED THIS NIGHT WITH US."

Becca read the entry out loud. "Thank you Josef," she murmured.

"Rebecca, would you do the honors?" Grandpa asked.

Becca sang the brachot as she lit the candles, then she turned to the opening of the Pesach service and began. "Now in the presence of loved ones and friends, before us the emblems of rejoicing, we gather for our sacred celebration. With the household of Israel, our elders and young ones, linking and bonding the past with the future, we heed once again the divine call to service. Living our story that is told for all peoples, whose shining conclusion is yet to unfold, we gather to observe the Passover, as it is written:"

And then Grandpa continued

"You shall keep the Feast of Unleavened Bread, for on this very day I brought your hosts out of Egypt. You shall observe this day throughout the generations as a practice for all times. We assemble in fulfillment of the mitzvah."

The sky faded to black. The gentle light of the candles was their only illumination. They continued to read, each taking a turn as the story unfolded. When they came to the matzah, Grandma said,

"This is the bread of distress, which our forefathers ate in Egypt. All who are hungry—let them come in and eat. All who are needy—let them come in and celebrate the Passover. For in the time of freedom, there is knowledge of servitude. And in the time of bondage, the hope of redemption."

She turned to Josef. "Now comes the best-known part, the four questions. Actually, it is one question with four answers. Will you read it for us?"

Josef nodded. He began to read and his musical voice made the words seem like magic.

"Why is this night different from all other nights?"

He paused, read ahead silently to himself, then looked up. He began again.

"Why is this night different from all other nights? For on all other nights, the bread of my plate had no meaning, but tonight it is a link to the past.

For on all other nights, I tasted the bitterness of defeat, with no hope for the future.

For on all other nights, the saltwater ocean was a prison, but tonight it offers escape.

For on all other nights, I have eaten to sustain my body, but tonight I sustain my soul."

A shiver passed through them all, but no one dared break the emotion of the moment by speaking their thoughts. And so they continued to read from the Haggadah, each passage revealing a newfound meaning.

When it was time for the meal, Grandma and Becca brought the bowls of steaming soup to the table. Three pairs of expectant eyes watched Grandpa as he ate.

At last he put down his spoon.

"So young man, you would like to continue your education."

"Yes sir. I would have to leave home for schooling, but my family needs my help."

"How much do you think you earn in a year?"

Josef wrinkled his forehead as he calculated his worth.

"Maybe three or four hundred dollars, U.S." he replied.

Becca gasped. Her airfare to Florida was that much.

Grandpa thought about this.

"If it isn't a financial burden, would your family allow you to go away for school?"

"It is their greatest dream, as well."

"You would need to meet the entrance standards, of course. And you'd probably be with students younger than yourself."

"I believe I could pass the exams. Becca could be my tutor. I can tell that she is very intelligent."

Becca blushed. "I'm not in high school yet," she said.

"Nonetheless, we could study together and practice the lessons. You would inspire me."

She laughed shyly. "I suppose I could help with some things."

"You can help me serve the fish," Grandma teased.

"Sure. No problem." Becca was glad for the diversion.

When the dishes had been changed and the rest of the meal served, they picked up the conversation.

"I've always been rather impressed with you son," Grandpa said. "I have no problem helping you financially. I can give your family the amount you would normally earn. Handling your living expenses would not be a burden. However, Maggie and I live on the Diaspora and we're never in one place for very long. You're not old enough for an apartment and I can't offer you a home."

"I understand," Josef said. He looked questioningly at Becca.

"We've only got three bedrooms. There wouldn't be room with us."

"I don't require much space," he replied hopefully.

She felt rather foolish. His home must be a tiny place, jammed with brothers and sisters.

Suddenly, she sat up very straight. "Grandma Ida!" she blurted out. "Grandma Ida and Grandpa Jake always have people staying with them. They had a Russian family just last year. There were four of them and they stayed a whole month. One boy wouldn't be a problem. Josef could even help Grandpa with the yard."

Now all the eyes were on her.

"I think you're right," Grandma said. "Ida's greatest joy is inviting people to her home."

"And she lives right in our neighborhood. I really could help Josef with his schoolwork."

Josef reached out and touched her hand. Becca felt a hot rush that started in her heart and shot up through her face right to the roots of her hair.

"But how can we ask your Grandmother for her permission?" he whispered hoarsely.

Becca had trouble speaking. She cleared her throat twice and turned to Grandpa.

"I guess we'd have to write a letter and wait for an answer. I suppose that would take too long."

"I think we can make our own Passover miracle," he laughed. "When you finish eating, we'll call her on the phone."

"Is there a public phone in the marina?" Becca asked. "We don't have one on board."

"Yes. There is a public phone, but we're going to call ship-to-shore from the Diaspora."

Becca had never eaten a Pesach meal as quickly as she did that night. They rushed through the closing prayers and skipped the singing altogether.

While Grandma washed the dishes, Grandpa sat at the nav station with Becca and Josef. Using the VHF radio, he reached the overseas operator. She forwarded the call to a United States operator, who connected them to their destination party.

Over the radio came the sound of a ringing phone. Grandpa handed the mike to Becca.

"Remember you're speaking over a radio frequency," he said. "Say 'Over' when you want the other person to talk."

Becca waited impatiently. Finally, she heard a click and her grandmother answered the phone.

"Hello?"

"Grandma! It's Becca. I'm calling from the boat. I'll say 'Over' when I want you to answer. Over."

"Rebecca, sweetheart." Grandma put her hand over the phone and called to the others. "It's Rebecca. She's calling from the boat.

"How are you baby?"

"Wonderful, Grandma. Really wonderful. We just had our seder. Grandma, I called because I have an important favor to ask from you and Grandpa. Over."

"For you, I always do favors. Is something wrong?"

"Of course not. I...that is we...know this boy who wants to go to school in the States. Grandpa George will pay for him, but he needs somewhere to live. Can he stay with you? Over."

"We always have room, especially for young people interested in knowledge. George and Maggie, they think this is a good idea?"

Grandpa took the microphone. "Hello Ida. It's George. Happy Pesach. Over."

"Thank you dear. Is your beautiful wife enjoying good health?"

"We're all fine, Ida. We can't talk for long. The radio signal usually fades. I heard your question and yes, we think it would be a good idea for the young man to live with you and go to school. Over."

"Then we will gladly do that mitzvah. When d...see...ca?"

Grandma's voice began to break up with static. Becca took the microphone back.

"Thank you Grandma. I'll see you soon. Over."

All she could hear in reply were incomprehensible bits and pieces. Grandpa reached over and switched it off.

"Congratulations young man," he said and shook Josef's hand. "Looks like your dream will come true."

Josef had the dazed look of a sleepwalker. He couldn't say anything, but kept shaking his head in disbelief.

"It's so hot in here," Grandma said. "Let's take our dessert and sit on deck." She handed wooden bowls of chocolate swirl ice cream to each of them, as they climbed up the stairs.

Becca took her bowl and walked to the bow. She sat down on the teakwood boards, her back against the mast.

Josef came up and leaned against the railing.

"Before today, I did not know your family were Jews," he said quietly. "I have never met any others, but I had heard that they only care for each other. Nothing could be further from the truth. That I can clearly see."

"Before today, I never thought much about the things I heard at Sunday School. I have a lot more to learn about being Jewish," Becca answered softly.

"Is it something anyone can learn?"

Becca laughed. "When you live with Grandma Ida, you'll learn about Judaism every day. That I can guarantee!"

"You are fortunate to have such wonderful grandparents."

"I think so, too. It's amazing! They are each very, very different. But, they are all very special."

"And their granddaughter is the same as they are. Intelligent. Caring. Beautiful."

Becca turned her head away. She suddenly felt shy again.

"The moon is full tonight," she said at last. "There's always a full moon on Passover."

The bright rays of the moon bounced off the waves and glimmered across the bay. They formed a wide silver band of light that pointed over the ocean to home.

# THE END